Our Fathers

A Novel
By
Jeff Collignon

ISBN: 978-0-6151-7274-3

Books by Jeff Collignon
Her Monster
Tropical Dark (with Walter Koenigstein)
A.S. (After Sarah)
Revelations

Writing as Borto Milan
In The Drift
Riding Towards Home

1

The first thing I notice about the woman is she's pregnant. The next is the M-16 she's got strapped to her back.

It's American issue.

Loony and I are crouched ten yards to the side of the trail. It's been raining all morning. We're both drenched.

Loony's breath catches in his throat as he spots the figure. Before I can turn to warn him, he screams and lights her up.

I watch the tight pattern of fire shred her belly. She falls on her back and flops in the mud.

Watching her die, all I feel is a small sense of relief that there's now one less person alive who might have killed me.

We return to base without encountering any more movement. Loony's still high from the rush of the kill. He keeps talking about Cleveland, gooks, and someone named Julia.

I let him run the report, knowing his version will be better than mine. His still carries some demented sense of duty. Mine would only be about survival.

As I pull off my boots, the left one rips away a two inch patch of skin from my instep. I stretch my toes and watch blood begin to ooze from the tear.

I'm lighting a cigarette when Clayton comes by.

"Fucking Laurel took one," he says, shaking his head in disgust. "Four fucking days in-country, and fucking new-guy Laurel gets a go-home special." He walks away, muttering angrily.

I smoke and study my feet. They don't even look like feet anymore. Swollen and mottled into a pale opalescence, they bear little resemblance to what they once were.

I pull my .45 and rest the barrel along the top of my knee. I click off the safety, take a bead on my foot, and hook the trigger.

After a long sweat filled moment, I holster my sidearm and slump against the wall. I hear a couple of guys laugh and look over to see them turning away, shaking their heads in disappointment.

I lie in my bunker and look at the sky. The stars here are different from The World. Here they seem much smaller and farther away.

I watch the sky until the flares start. Red going out, green coming in.

Small arms fire starts next. No one puts a lot into it, they just pop off rounds to let everyone know they're still here.

I pull out the letter I started to my brother. Light from the multi-colored flares flickers across the page. I read the last sentence I wrote yesterday morning: *I don't want to die here.* And can't think of much else to add.

I pull a can of beer from my pack and drink half of it, then lean over the sandbags and fire a few rounds into the darkness. I hear someone laughing near the perimeter, and can't tell if it's one of us or one of them.

There's too many ways to die. It's not just them, it's also us. No one knows what the hell anyone is doing anymore, and everyone just keeps doing something, hoping it might be the right thing. Over in the 47th, they sent out a recon unit, three hours later someone called in an air strike. They wiped out the whole unit. No one knows who made the call, and no one seems to care enough to find out.

There doesn't seem to be any reason to be here. We kill them. They kill us. And it just keeps going on, until it's all numbers and body bags. I think...

"INCOMING," someone shouts.

I dive to the bottom of the bunker. The fetid odor of the earth swamps around me. I inhale, pulling the scent into my lungs as the ground around me shudders and groans.

The groan changes pitch until it becomes a scream of agony.

The scream goes on. Our howitzers start to return fire. The sky lights up like a rainbow. A chorus of small arms and .50 cal tracers joins in to accompany the ululation.

I lie on my back and stare at the sky and wait for the song to end.

2

John built his fort in the woods behind our house. If it weren't for the noise, I never would have found it.

"What do you want?" He's sitting on a branch, six feet above my head.

"I want to come up."

"You're too little."

"Am not."

"You're only eight. You have to be ten to come up here."

"What's that noise?"

"What noise?"

I can tell by his face he's hiding something. I know about hiding things.

"If you don't let me come up, I'll tell."

"Tell what?"

"What you're doing."

"I'm not doing anything."

I start to walk away.

"Wait!"

I'm smiling when I turn. I stop when I see my brother's face.

"If you come up, you have to keep it a secret."

Another secret, I think happily. Like the secret eyes my mother hides behind her sunglasses, or the murky bottles my father keeps hidden in the garage.

He kicks down a rope. I wrap my arms and legs around the rough hemp and shinny up.

A sheet of warped plywood makes up the floor of the fort. The sides are made out of the cardboard box Mrs. Mays new refrigerator came in.

"This is nice. This is..." I stop when I hear the noise. It's the same sound that led me into the woods, a high pitched keening sound. John is crouched in the corner, hiding something behind his back.

"What'd you have?"

"Nothing."

"C'mon, I won't tell."

"You promise."

"I promise."

He steps aside. The William's dog is in the corner. It's lying on its side. A rag is tied around its muzzle, and its legs are tied together with shoe laces.

"That's Prince, isn't it?" I start forward then stop, one of the dog's eyes is broken. I look at my brother. "You did that?"

"Yes."

"Why?"

He shrugs and nudges the dog with his foot.

Prince whimpers.

"You better let him go. If Mr. Williams finds out, he'll tell dad."

"So what?"

"So dad'll get mad."

"He's always mad."

"But he'll get madder."

"How could he get any more mad?" John wonders.

We wrap the rope around Prince and lower him to the ground. I untie him, because John's afraid he'll bite him.

I talk to him softly as I pull the rag from his muzzle, to let him know I love him. He doesn't bite me when I pull it off.

As soon as his legs are free, he darts into the woods. I stand beside my brother, beneath his fort in the woods, and listen to the dog's cries as he runs home.

It's Monday night. My father bowls every Monday night. It's our favorite night of the week.

My mother is making tuna casserole for dinner. My father hates tuna fish.

John and I stay in the kitchen and talk to her as she cooks. She smiles a lot, and once she even reaches over to touch my brother's shoulder.

Sometimes I think Monday nights might be my mother's favorite night, too.

We eat in the kitchen at the small formica table. I can feel the hard press of my brother's leg on one side, and the soft fullness of my mother's on the other.

After dinner we help my mother do the dishes. John's two years older, so he gets to wash. I only get to dry. My mother hums as she clears the table.

When she's finished, she leans against the stove and asks us questions about school.

When it's my turn to answer, I tell her not only what happened that day, but everything that happened throughout the week.

I stop when I see her smile, then turn to catch the same smile on my brother's face.

I wonder if my smile looks like theirs.

We sit on the couch and watch TV. My mother sits in the middle. We snuggle against her, until she says, "C'mon, you two, give me a little room to breathe."

John glares at me until I move away.

We watch Have Gun Will Travel. John knows all the words to the Paladin song and sings along. My mother smiles and touches his hair. I don't know the words, but I start to sing, too. I make up what I don't know.

"Okay, boys, time for bed," my mother announces, as Paladin rides into the desert.

I go into the bathroom first. I practice smiling as I brush my teeth.

John yells at me to hurry up.

I spit, rinse, smile, then step out of the bathroom. John rolls his eyes and steps around me. I hear the solid click of the lock as I walk into the living room.

I kiss my mother good night. Her cheek is smooth and cool. She smells of cigarette smoke and coffee. A man on TV says:

'Twenty two military advisors arrived in Indochina today. "Their stay will be a brief one," President Eisenhower assured reporters. Senator John Fitzgerald Kennedy announced his first campaign choice this afternoon. His brother Bobby Kennedy will be..."

"Bed." My mother nudges me with her foot.

At the top of the stairs I look back to see my brother leaning over to kiss my mother's cheek. I turn away when she reaches up to hug him.

By the time John comes into the bedroom, I'm already in bed. I watch as he undresses, puts on his pajamas, then pulls his flashlight from beneath his mattress. He turns off the overhead light then flicks on his flashlight. I hear the pages of his book rustling softly.

"What're you reading?"

"A book."

"What book?"

"A good one. Now go to sleep."

"I'm not tired."

"Then don't go to sleep, just leave me alone."

I hear the murmur of the TV downstairs. I hold my breath when I hear a car come up our street. I breathe again when it passes our house.

"John?"

"What?"

"How come daddy's so mean?"

"Because he can be."

"Is that why you did that to Prince's eye, because you can be mean, too?"

"I don't like Prince."

"Maybe daddy doesn't like us," I say fearfully.

"No," John answers. "He love us."

"He loves mommy, too, doesn't he?"

"Yes, now go to sleep."

I turn on my side to face the wall.

I fall asleep to the sound of the pages of my brother's book turning behind me.

3

"I fucked up," Loony groans.

I roll over to see him sitting on the edge of my bunker.

"What?" I croak, hunching forward, trying to pull out of the dream.

He hands me a cup of coffee.

I can't remember the dream, but my father was in it. As I cradle the coffee to my chest, I remember my father's eyes, the way he looked at me.

Loony scratches the side of his jaw and says, "I got a little carried away yesterday."

"How carried away?"

He shrugs, cracks his knuckles, then shakes his head. "Way the fuck carried away."

I sip the lukewarm coffee and wait him out.

"I told Harrison we took out a supply line."

"Oh shit!"

"I thought he might give us R&R or something." He pulls a pack of cigarettes, takes out two, straightens them, passes me one.

"He thinks we're hot shit now. He wants us to run recon into Son Ha."

"When?"

"Tonight," Loony says. He tries to laugh, chokes. His eyes fasten on mine. "What the fuck we going to do?"

"I don't know," I reply, thinking I'd better finish the letter to my brother.

Son Ha is about thirty klicks inland, southeast of Quang Ngai. It's all mountains, hills, and bush. The Viet Minh have been there forever. We'd been getting reports recently that the Cong had moved into the area as well. We'd been trying to sweep the region for the last three months without any success. Sending us in, seemed at the very least desperate, and at worst futile.

After Dexter blew up, I'd been passed all the way up to C&C with my request.

I'd ended up standing in front of George Meola, a G-3.

I was still wearing the same fatigues I'd worn on patrol. Dexter's blood had long since stiffened and dried. The whole left side of my uniform was plastered to my body with blown-up bits of Dexter and the two other men he'd taken with him.

"I want to go out alone," I'd told the C&C.

"That's not the way we operate here."

"Then I want to go home."

Meola laughed. He sobered when he realized I was serious.

"I could court martial you for that."

"Yes, sir, I know, but it wouldn't kill me."

He leaned back in his chair to study me. He shook his head wearily, then told me to get the fuck out of his sight.

Two days later I was transferred to LRRP school.

What I'd discovered early in The Nam was other people could get you killed. Didn't matter whose side they were on. One mistake was all it took. Dexter had taught me that lesson. It was a valuable one, and one I was determined to remember.

There were always looking for volunteers for Long Range Reconnaissance Patrols. The LRRPS were made up of a hundred and fifty men who usually operated in five man teams, less if they'd taken casualties.

The training was brutal, and only a small percentage of applicants ever made it to graduation. Most of the volunteers were attracted by the hard core mystique, but all I cared about were the perks that came with being a LRRP. No one wore rank, no one saluted, and you operate a week in-country and a week out. You were even allowed to carry your weapon on base.

As dangerous as Long Range Recon was reputed to be, I was sure it couldn't be any worse than humping trails with Fucking New Guys like Dexter.

"I tried to talk to him," Loony explains. We're slouched against the side of the PX. We each have a can of beer and a cigarette burning.

I lean against the wall and stretch out my legs. The hot sand feels good on my heels. I can almost feel the sun sucking out the moisture and pus from my feet.

"Didn't do any good. He said we'd only been out for a half a day."

I nod, too comfortable to speak. Moments of quiet sanity were too rare to ruin with words.

"Then I tried to tell him that after last week there was only the two of us left." He hawks up a mouthful of phlegm and spits. "He said there ain't nobody else to go."

A puff of smoke plumes the sky in the eastern quadrant. An instant later I hear the sound of the explosion.

"RPG," Loony says idly, eyeing the drifting smoke.

I draw my legs to my chest to examine my feet as our 81's start to return fire.

The skin along the bottom of each foot is wrinkled and white. The tear along the instep has stopped oozing. If I could keep them out another day, I know they'd be all right.

I lean back and try not to think about what it's going to feel like tonight when I have to pull on my boots.

I wobble to my feet when Loony starts in about the Geneva Accords again.

"C'mon, man, don't you want to talk about this shit?" he says, shading his eyes to look at me.

I flex my toes in the sand, then shake my head and turn away.

I hear him call out, but I keep walking.

I sit alongside a Huey, long since requisitioned by Medevac. It's surface is punctured with shell fragments, and blossoming from each hole are sharp, jagged petals. A dark, tacky stain has coagulated in the sand around the skids.

I have the letter to my brother in my lap. I read it, unable to remember when I wrote most of it. It seems as if I've been writing it for months.

...the only real thing about this place is the fear, and figuring out how to deal with it. I used to think it was just the fear itself that incapacitated. But I don't believe that anymore. If anything, it's the exact opposite.

Two weeks ago we found a marine outside of Da Nang after Charlie had gotten through with him. They'd cut off his hands and feet, and then shoved a bamboo rod up his rectum until it punctured his stomach. They'd left him lying outside an abandoned village.

When they'd left him, he was alive.

When we found him, he was long dead.

There's nothing that can prepare you for something like that. It's way beyond anyone's imagination.

This whole thing isn't about God, duty, or country. It's all about fear, and how to live with it, deal with it, and find some way to make it your friend.

I shift my legs into the sunlight and stretch out my right foot. The skin cracks and begin to bleed.

Blood is good. It means it's finally starting to heal.

I dreamed about him last night. I can't remember the dream. I only remember the way his eyes looked.

Bullet eyes, we use to call them. Maybe that's what made me think of him.

I'm not afraid of him anymore. Even if he was still alive, I don't think I'd be afraid of him. There's too much else to be afraid of. All of his rage and insanity seems pretty small to what the world has to offer now.

Does he still scare you?

I hear Loony call out and look up to see him walking over with a six pack of beer.

I put the letter away and reach for a beer.

He sits beside me and shakes his head. "Fucking Accords, man."

"Fucking A," I agree, and raise my beer.

I listen to Loony's disjointed ramblings about a moment in history that would eventually prove to rule our lives.

"Fucking French," he says. "They killed us."

"All of us," I reply wearily.

The sun is directly overhead. It seems to momentarily pause in preparation for its descent.

When it touches the western tree line, Loony and I will disappear into the bush, onto the other side of the world.

4

I sit in the front of the bus with Bobby Shore. John sits in the back with Johnny May and Randy Connel.

"We got a new car," Bobby tells me.

I don't know anything about cars, but I pretend I do as Bobby talks about the size of the engine and the amount of horsepower.

When the bus stops in front of the school, I step to the side. Randy and Johnny come out first. John comes last.

"Mr. Shore got a new car," I whisper.

John nods, but doesn't say anything. He likes to pretend he doesn't know me at school. I don't know why.

"C'mon!" Bobby yells.

We race around to the playground. We each shinny up one of the basketball poles and touch the net.

I spot Nancy Helke looking up at us.

"Hey!" she yells. "I want to come up, too."

"You have to wait your turn," Bobby tells her.

"Well, hurry up, the bell's going to ring."

Bobby reaches over and hangs from the net. When Nancy starts up the pole, he quickly swings back and grins down at her.

I slide to the pavement and step back without saying anything.

Nancy looks at me then grabs the pole and starts to climb.

As she climbs, I see a pale flicker of white fabric between her bare legs.

The bell rings.

Bobby slides down and runs across the playground.

I wait for Nancy's feet to touch the ground before I start to walk away.

"Hey!"

I turn to see her looking at me.

She brushes back her bangs and smiles. An instant later she darts across the playground and disappears into the school.

Mrs. Sherwood hates me. She hated John too when she had him in her class. John told me he thinks it's because she's crazy.

I sit in the back next to Bill Boyer. She likes Bill.

"And the capitol of our state is?"

"Springfield," we all say in unison.

Mrs. Sherwood smiles. Her smile disappears as she points at me. She never says my name. She only points.

"What's the capitol of Oregon. Quick?"

"Salem."

"And North Dakota?"

"Pierre."

She makes a face and looks at Bill. "Bill, tell us what the capitol of North Dakota is?"

"Bismarck," he says.

"Pay attention," she warns me, then goes back to Geography.

She leaves me alone for the rest of the day.

Bobby Shore saves a seat for me on the bus.

I look for Nancy. She's sitting three seats behind me with Joanne Alborne. They're both laughing.

Bobby asks if I want to come over to see their new car.

Bobby is eight months older than I am. He lives with his little brother Tommy four blocks from our house. His house is light grey and doesn't have a garage.

"Where will you keep your new car?" I ask as we climb out of the bus.

"Outside."

"You should build a garage, so it doesn't get all dirty."

"Maybe I'll ask my father."

"I'm going over to Bobby's to see his new car," I tell John.

Johnny and Randy are standing with him, so John just shrugs and turns away.

"I don't like Johnny," Bobby whispers.

"How come?"

"He's a jerk."

"He's my brother's best friend."

"I don't like your brother either." Bobby grins.

His smile looks just like Mrs. Sherwood's.

"Where you going?"

"You can keep your old car," I yell.

"I like him," Bobby shouts. "I like John."

I run down to the lake. The best way to get there is to cut through Klimas's Resort. There's a hill behind the Resort that leads down to the water. In the winter, we go sledding down the hill. We have contests to see who can go the farthest. On the edge of Klimas's property is an old wire fence with lots of holes. On the other side of the fence are three summer homes, then Mr. Welty's. After Mr. Welty's property, there's a place where people keep their boats. It's where my father keeps his row boat.

No one is supposed to walk on the other side of the fence because it's private property, but I always do. The only person who ever yells at me is Mr. Welty, and that's only because he's worried about his flowers. When I come to his property, I always run across it real fast so he can't catch me.

The summer house next to Mr. Welty's has a small pier. It's my favorite place. I like to sit at the end of the pier and watch the lake. Sometimes I can see fish jumping. I told my father about them once. I thought he might want to try to catch them, but he got mad at me for being on private property.

I don't tell him about the fish anymore.

Mr. Welty lives alone. His wife died two years ago of cancer. My mother always whispers when she says this. I think it must have hurt a lot.

I watch Mr. Welty's house until I'm sure no one's around, then race across the property. By the time I reach the other side I'm out of breath. I crouch over and look back at Mr. Welty's house. It's white with green windows. Maple trees grow on each side, and in back there is an oak tree and a giant weeping willow tree.

The house always seems empty. Even when I know Mr. Welty is inside, it seems empty. It makes me sad to see his house. I don't know why. Maybe it's because of all the flowers.

I start up the hill to our house. I'm kicking a can so I don't look up until I'm right in front of it.

My father's car in the driveway.

I look at it for a long time before I walk to the back door and go into the kitchen.

"He's home," John whispers. He has a glass of milk and a chocolate chip cookie. I hear my parents voices in the living room.

"Is he mad?"

"Not yet."

"I want a cookie."

"They're in the stove."

My mother always hides the cookies. John is very good at finding them. She never gets mad when he does. She only smiles and says next time she'll find a better place.

I get a cookie and walk over to the refrigerator for a glass of milk.

"Don't spill," John warns.

My father gets mad when we spill. It makes me nervous John said that. I close the refrigerator door and get a glass of water instead. It doesn't taste the same, but it's safer.

I look at John when I hear my father's footsteps. He winces, then ducks his head.

I turn to see my father in the doorway.

He's smiling.

I smile back and say hi.

"How you doing, Scout," he says, and ruffles my hair.

I giggle, then find I can't stop.

John shakes his head at me.

"What'd you do to your brother," my father says to John. "Give him the giggling disease."

I start laughing even harder. I spit out a piece of cookie on the table.

"Lets not get too carried away," my father cautions.

I stop laughing.

John is staring at the table.

I hunch my shoulders until I hear my father walk over to the refrigerator. He pulls out a bottle of beer and carries it to the sink.

He grabs a glass, fills it, then turns to watch us.

I keep staring at the bottle in his hand. John nudges me with his foot. I look at him and he shakes his head.

My father nods, then leaves the kitchen.

I take a deep breath and look across the table. John has his eyes closed and is leaning back in his chair.

We have to finish our homework before dinner. I have arithmetic and geography to do. John says he has to make a book report.

My father is in his chair in the corner of the living room beside the fireplace. He's reading the newspaper. He holds it in front of him so I can't see his face. He folds the newspaper on his lap and reaches for his glass of beer. As he raises it to his mouth, his eyes settle on me.

I scurry up the stairs into our room.

John is on his bed reading his book.

I flop on my bed and watch him read.

"How come he's home?"

"Mom said he got off early."

"Is he going to be home all night?"

John shrugs.

"You think he'll go to Klimas's tonight?"

"How do I know." He shakes his head and holds his book in front of his face.

He holds it the same way my father holds the newspaper.

I finish my homework first. John is still reading. I look out the window at the field behind our house. In the center of the field is an old apple tree. A path starts at the back of our house and cuts through the field all the way out to the tree. Bobby Shore and I play war there. Mr. Shore was in the Korean War so Bobby knows a lot about war. It's his favorite game.

I lie down on the floor and slide over to the doorway.

My father is in his chair. My mother is in front of the fireplace. They're talking, but I can't hear what they're saying.

"What are they doing?"

"Talking."

"Does he look mad?"

I examine my father's face.

My father's hair is all gray. My mother says this makes him look distinguished. He has hairy eyebrows, green eyes, and a long chin. My mother says he is very handsome.

When he's mad, his lips get tight and his eyes turn into bullets.

I look at his eyes closely.

"I don't think so."

"Are you sure?"

"A little sure."

John makes a face, then picks up his book and starts to read.

I slide across the floor beneath my bed. My blanket hangs over the edge. I pretend I'm in a tent in the jungle, and there are ferocious animals outside who will eat me if I come out.

5

"No insertion," Loony tells me. "They want us to walk in."

I shake my head and go back to studying the aerial photos and Recon files.

We're outside the Armory, sitting against the side of the building with our legs splayed out in front of us. The sun is lying low in the sky. A couple of grunts stop in front of us. One of them looks at our legs, then looks at me. He opens his mouth. The other grabs him by the arm, shakes his head, says "Lurps."

They walk around us.

"Going to be a bitch," Loony says, jamming his finger into the map, at the Son Ha area.

After examining the terrain, and reading the Recon updates about enemy movement, I say, "Yeah, maybe we'd better stay home."

Loony laughs and pulls a cigarette.

I wonder if he knows I'm serious.

As the sun touches the top of the tree line, we gear up.

We're carrying M-16s, .45 sides, signal instructions, first aid packs, eight canteens, M-16 pouches and magazines, 2 six foot lengths of Swiss rope, groundsheets, maps, K-bars, mirrors, compasses, d'rings, towels, ponchos, gloves, a spare set of fatigues, extra socks, notebooks, 2 PRC-25 radios, 2 extra batteries, entrenching tools, trip flares, star clusters, grenades, smoke grenades, claymores, binoculars, gas masks, and insect repellent.

Between us we're packing a little under two hundred pounds. We're suppose to move through the bush quickly and quietly.

I pull my boots on last. My feet immediately begin to swell.

Lt. Harrison comes by to do a final check. He stands behind us and examines our rucksacks, then steps in front to check our weapons.

"Any problems?"

We shake our heads.

He nods. We start to turn.

"Wait a minute." He plants himself in front of us, then reaches into Loony's pocket and pulls out a pack of cigarettes.

"Get the fuck out of here," he says, shaking his head in disgust.

We move into the bush, following the shadows. The land quickly swallows us.

A hundred yards out of base, we pull up beside a pile of rocks.

Grunting, Loony dumps his rusack to the ground and steps over to the mound.

"Kick it first," I caution, slipping out of my pack.

As he pulls back his leg, I see a sinuous flash of green slither into the brush.

"I hate this fucking place," Loony groans, and drops to his knees in front of the mound.

We clear away the rocks to uncover a three by two foot trench. Two groundsheets cover the top of the hole.

Loony pulls off the groundsheets as I begin unloading our packs.

After looting it all of the drugs, we dump one of the first aid kits then discard one groundsheet, both sets of fatigues, gloves, and entrenching tools, trip flares, star clusters, smoke grenades, binoculars, and gas masks.

"What do you think?" Loony holds up the extra PRC-25 radio.

"Fuck it, no one's going to miss us."

He unpacks it, along with the spare battery.

I pull two pump .12 gauge shotguns from the trench, along with extra ammo for our M-16s and .45s We have the ammo rigged up in socks, which we hang from our utility belts.

I reach into the trench and pull out the letter I've been writing to my brother. It's packed in a plastic bag, along with sixty hits of dextroamphetamine tablets.

Loony reaches in and pulls out four packs of cigarettes. He lights one as we repack the trench with our discarded equipment.

Thirty minutes later we're ready to move. We're down to fifty pounds a piece. I feel fast and light.

I take a hit of the Dex, then pass one to Loony. I hear him chewing as we start to move out.

We do nothing the school way. There's a whole list of Recon regs which neither of us follows. Harrison knows this, but plays along with our game. What keeps him going along with our game, is we're both still alive.

We're okay for three klicks. We know the ground. There's nothing here that scares us.

Loony's even got a cigarette bobbing from his lips. I catch an occasional glimpse of the burning tip out the corner of my eye.

The flat-lands end abruptly at the lip of a valley. A sliver of moon casts an eerie spray of light along the twisted trees and thick brush trailing down the side of the depression.

Crouching at the edge, we scan the bush ahead and below. A cloud of mosquitoes swarm us. The repellent's only good for a couple of hours. The insects buzz my eyes, darting in and out, waiting to feed.

Loony nudges me and nods to the valley.

I nod back, feeling the first touch of fear, feeling its hunger begin to grow.

Keeping low, we scuttle forward and slip over the edge of the world.

Greasy perspiration beads along my forehead and runs into my eyes as we move into the trees, into the darkness. The smell of damp earth and moss fills my nostrils. Water drips from the branches onto my shoulders. My fatigues are soaked and stick to my back and legs. The humidity sucks the moisture from my body.

Loony's eyes peer at me from the shadows. His eyes seem inhumanly large.

The mud sucks at my feet. I carry the shotgun in my right hand. Loony carries his 16. We alternate weapons.

I like the shotgun. It blows up everything in sight. The 16 requires an element of skill I don't trust. I prefer obliteration over accuracy.

When we hit the floor of the valley, we both freeze before we're even aware we're going to stop. I feel the rhythmic rush of blood through my temples, hear the ravenous drone of mosquitoes.

Loony looks at me, then slowly reaches up to touch the side of his nose.

I inhale, catching the scent. I nod, then drop to my stomach and inch forward. I stop at the edge of the brush. Thirty yards in front of me is a small village. It appears deserted. No smoke rises from any of the hooches. No sign of movement.

Without turning, I move my left foot from side to side.

Loony edges up. I shake my head at him.

He touches his nose again.

I take a deep breath, catalogue the odors, then shake my head insistently.

Loony's eyes bore into mine.

I clench my teeth, nod curtly, then turn away.

I start across the clearing. Loony stays behind, covering me.

The moonlight cast the village in a benign light. It seems to soften all the edges and tries to lure me into a false sense of security.

I stop at the side of one of the hooches. A window is directly above me. It's a dark mouth opening into more darkness.

I ease up the wall, then dart a glance inside.

I sag to the ground, feeling the sweat cool on my body.

We sit in one of the abandoned huts. Loony carefully cups a match and lights a cigarette. He inhales, covering the tip with both hands, then holds it out to me.

I take a hit, feeling the fear recede, coiling along the pit of my stomach.

We move out of the village and start across the floor of the ravine. The land begins to rise. The ground grows rockier. Only the sound of our breath marks our passing.

A little before first light we reach the other side of the valley. A thick stand of trees rises along its edge. Behind the trees is a stretch of hills, gradually leading up into the mountains.

Loony stops. He moves his hand from side to side, then points to the trees.

I scan the area. The shadows are beginning to lengthen as a bright shaft of light slices across the eastern horizon.

I nod and push forward.

We move into the trees.

The sun is fully in the sky by the time we tie off. We're twenty feet in the air, tied to the trunk of a tree. A canopy of leaves and branches hides the ground. The limbs rise up around each side of us, offering us additional cover.

We're each seated on a thick branch, on opposites sides of the tree. We're tied to the trunk with a single length of rope. Our packs are hung within easy reach.

All of Loony's movements are telegraphed to me through the rope binding us to the trunk.

I pull two freeze dried packs of chicken stew from my rusack. I eat mine dry. I hear Loony mixing his with water.

When we're done, I replace the empties in my pack.

Loony lights a cigarette. The sweet odor of the smoke drifts over to me. I feel the rope cut into my waist as he inhales. A moment later it digs in more sharply.

I reach to my side and take the cigarette. I draw the smoke deep into my lungs, then carefully stub it out, cupping my hand to catch the ash.

I lean back and close my eyes. The land slowly unravels in my mind.

The stale scent of the village, the fecund odor of the mud, the pungent stink of my own terror.

I open my eyes. The sun splinters through the leaves, boring into my chest. My feet throb and itch. The flesh feels inflamed and swollen.

I escape into the darkness waiting behind my eyes. The rope suddenly shifts. I wait, holding my breath, then relax and slip back into the darkness, welcoming it, finding a small measure of safety in its emptiness.

6

After John falls asleep, I tip toe over to his bed. His book is lying on the pillow beside him. I carry it to the doorway and sit beneath the hall light.

David and the Phoenix is what it's called. I open it to the first page and start to read.

I'm standing in the field beneath the apple tree. I hear something moving through the weeds. I duck behind the tree and listen.

I hear someone begin to cry. I move to the edge of the field and look out at the dark path. Something rustles behind me. It's the apple tree.

It's moving.

It's reaching for me.

I try to run but my feet are frozen.

I hear someone laughing.

"Daddy!" I scream.

"What are you doing?" John is crouched beside me.

I'm lying on the floor. I can't remember where I am. It scares me. I try not to cry.

He takes my hand and leads me to my bed. I climb beneath the covers. John pulls them up to my chin.

"I was in the field," I whisper.

"It was just a dream."

My hand is lying outside the covers.

John picks up my hand and pushes it beneath the blanket.

"Go to sleep now, it's late."

"The apple tree tried to eat me."

"I won't let anything eat you," he promises.

I nod, keeping my lower lip between my teeth.

"John?" I call a few moments later.

"Yeah?"

"Nothing," I say, then turn on my side, and watching him, fall asleep.

My parent's bedroom is at the bottom of the stairs. When no one is around I like to sneak inside and look in their drawers.

The top three drawers are my father's. The bottom three are my mother's.

My father keep his underwear and handkerchiefs in his top drawer. His underwear is very large. It fits over the outside of my pants and still falls down.

He keeps his work shirts in the next drawer. They are all white, and they come wrapped in plastic with gray pieces of cardboard behind them.

In his third drawer are two pairs of jeans and one pair of brown pants. He wears the brown pants when he works in the garden. The knees have dark stains all over them.

My mother's drawers are strange. Her top and bottom one have shirts and pants in them, but the middle one has things I've never seen my mother wear. Some of it is underwear, but there are other things with straps and clips I don't understand.

I like to lie on their bed and put my face in their pillows. My father's pillow smells like shaving and smoke.

My mother's smells like flowers.

Once I found a dime and two quarters behind their dresser. I hid the money under my pillow until I was sure no one knew it was gone. I bought Bit O Honeys and Cokes with the money. John kept asking me where I got it, but I just told him I found it. I didn't tell him where.

When my father is walking, he likes to put his hands in his pocket and play with his change. I can always tell where he is by the sound he makes.

My mother is much quieter. I never know where she is.

My grandfather is very old. He is my father's father. He came to visit us last summer. My mother said he was very sad because his wife died. He never looked sad to me. He would always smile and give me a nickel.

He and my father would sit on the front lawn and drink beer. Once I hid behind the lilac bushes to see what they were saying.

"God dammit, dad, it's none of your business," I heard my father say. It sounded strange to hear him say dad. I wondered if his dad called him Scout when he was little.

"You've seen what it's done to me. How can you let the same thing happen to you?"

"I've got it under control." My father finished his beer and reached for another.

"I don't think you have," my grandfather said softly.

"Well, to be perfectly honest, dad, I don't give a shit what you think," my father said, then rose and went into the house. I waited to see what my grandfather would do.

First he lit a cigarette, then he opened another beer.

When I snuck back into the house, my father was waiting for me..

"Where the hell have you been!" His lips were tight.

"Outside," I mumbled.

"Get to bed. It's late," he growled, then picked up his beer.

As I passed my parent's room, I heard my mother crying on the other side of the door.

After school, I walk into the woods to my brother's fort.

"What do you want?"

"I want to come up."

He's holding my father's fishing knife.

"Where'd you get that?"

"Why? You going to tell?"

"I won't tell."

He studies me for a moment, then kicks down the rope.

"Can I hold it?"

"Don't break it," he warns, then passes me the knife.

It has a black handle with a white circle in the center. The blade is as long as my hand.

"I got it out of his fishing box."

"He'd kill you if he found out."

"How's he going to find out?" John looks at me suspiciously.

I shrug, then close the blade. It clicks solidly in place.

"Is it sharp?"

He takes the knife and saws away a small branch. He holds it up to show me.

"What're you going to do with it?"

John walks around to the front of his fort.

Prince is in the corner, tied to the trunk of the tree.

John kneels in front of him.

"Don't hurt him!"

John looks over his shoulder.

I kick the side of the fort and wait to see what he's going to do.

"C'mere, boy." He holds out his hand.

Prince takes a small step and licks his fingers.

John pets the back of his head.

Prince's one eye is looking at me. I walk over and pet her, too.

"You've been a bad dog," John says and sticks the knife in Prince's front paw.

Prince squeals and tries to scramble away.

"Hold him!" John shouts.

I can feel the dog's heart thudding against my hand.

"Now it's your turn." He hands me the knife.

I run my thumb over the blade. It's very sharp.

Prince is bleeding. There are bloody paw prints on the floor of the fort.

"Do it," he whispers.

When I look at him, I'm afraid he's going to start to cry. I've only seen John cry once, and when I did it made me cry, too.

I take the knife and hold it over Prince's paw.

Prince twists his head to look at me. His one eye seems very large.

"Bad dog," John says softly. His breath hitches in his throat.

Prince whimpers and tries to scamper away.

I hear my brother sob.

I drop the knife and run out of the fort.

7

It's late September. I'm sitting in class. Dr. Miles is lecturing.

The sun is shining through the windows. It splashes across my desk. A fly circles above my head.

Dr. Miles makes a disparaging remark about President Johnson, about the war. Everyone laughs.

He talks about Southeast Asia, begins outlining the early occupation by the French and the French Accords.

I lean back in my chair. The dusty smell of chalk and the scent of clean, unbroken bodies fills my nostrils.

The screech of metal gains my attention. I look up to see Dr. Miles staring in horror at the door.

"What are you..." Before he can complete the sentence, a burst of fire shreds his chest. Like some conjurers trick, a bright array of red flowers blossoms from his white shirt.

A girl screams. I hear the metallic snap of another clip being loaded and hit the floor. I roll across the classroom, desperately searching for my weapon...

I wake, covered in greasy sweat. The sun pierces through the branches, drilling into me.

I take a deep breath, then freeze as I hear movement below.

Using only my stomach muscles I strain against the rope, until I feel a corresponding reaction from Loony.

Feeling a rush of blood thudding through my wrists and temples, I peer through the leaves.

I see them before I hear them. Five of them in sight, and more out of my line of vision. Their voices rise up the trunk of the tree. The words are incomprehensible, but the unwieldy language is easily identifiable.

The rope tightens. Loony touches my side. I reach for his hand and hold it. His fingers grip mine painfully.

We become a part of the tree.

Ants pepper my neck and cheeks. I feel them moving beneath my clothes, gnawing into my flesh.

The sun is pitiless. It presses against me, suffocating me. Sweat beads across my face and drips down my chin onto my chest.

I hang on to the scream. It builds again and again in the back of my throat, and each time I promise myself that next time I'll be able to let it loose.

It's late afternoon before the VC finally pack up and move out. We hear the clamor of their weapons and then only silence.

The rope relaxes around me. Loony's hand disappears from mine, leaving a cold sheen of perspiration coating my palm.

When we climb down, there are no visible signs of their ever having been there.

"2nd Regiment?" Loony whispers. "Should we call it in?"

I nod, then gesture to the west.

We move out of the trees and start to climb the low lying hills. We find shelter in a stand of bamboo.

Loony sets up the PRC, while I take the perimeter. I crouch on the lip of the hill, scanning the bush. Behind me I hear Loony's frantic whisper, outlining our coordinates.

As soon as he signs off, we quickly pack up and move. We take cover when we hear the Bandits coming in from the South.

Cowering along an incline, we watch the Hueys light up the valley. Tracers shred the trees. Huge splinters of wood and debris explode across the horizon.

Their fire is not exact. I watch as a 2.75 obliterates the stand of bamboo where we made contact.

Dexter had been in-country three weeks, and had survived two patrols. He was at that point where no one wanted anything to do with him. He was starting to feel cocky. He was losing that edge of fear that makes survival possible.

Four klicks out from base, Dexter hit a Betty. I was right behind him. I heard the click of the spring, saw a blur of movement rising in front of him.

"Oh shit!" I heard Dexter groan, as I dove to the ground, rolling forward, trying to get beneath the charge.

It cut Dexter in half, and took out the two men behind me.

I listened to their screams as I wiped the blood from my eyes and saw them writhing in the mud, limbs missing, blood spurting from their bodies.

What happens to all the butchered we send home? Where do they all go? What do they do?

We eat some dex and move out. The hills grow around us. When we're not climbing, we're moving through brush that confront us like a wall. We have to cut our way through it.

The palms of my hands are bleeding. The machete keeps slipping through my fingers. My boots are saturated, tightening around my swollen feet. Sweat drips into my eyes. My pack cuts into my back and shoulders. The weight of it seems to increase with every step.

Loony drops into a crouch.
I slither up beside him.

The smell of rot surrounds us.   Three bodies are splayed across the side of a hill.

Loony holds up two fingers, pauses, then holds up one. His eyes cling to mine.

I study the bodies, spot the lone American, then nod.

I point to the hill, look at Loony, then start to move.

The first gook's face is gone. He took direct fire. Ants and flies have burrowed in the carnage.

I turn away when I spot a slither of movement in the decaying flesh of his chest.

The other gook seems untouched. His face is in quiet repose as if he were sleeping.

The third body is one of ours. I motion to Loony and wait for him to step back before I start to move around the soldier, carefully examining the ground and his clothes.

Loony waits for my nod before he kneels beside the American. I step out of range and watch as he slowly begins to remove the dog tags. I hear a tearing sound as the metal peels away from the dried blood around the soldier's neck.

Loony pockets the tags as I set grenades around the bodies.

As we move away, the scent of putrefaction follows us. It clings to our clothes, reminding us of its morbid promise.

By mid day we're coming into the mountains. We burrow in to the jungle, moving into the elephant grass. The stalks slither through our fingers, leaving shallow cuts. I pull the antibiotic ointment from my pack, coat my hands and wrists, then pass the tube to Loony.

Pock time. Charlie lays back and rests, takes his afternoon nap so he can wake refreshed and ready to kill again. Charlie will set his perimeter with trail watchers and stationary outposts.

It's too easy to stumble into him. Its one of the few Recon regs we always follow.

We eat freeze dried beef hash, and kill off a canteen of water.

Loony reaches into his pocket and pulls a cigarette.

I lunge for his arm and hang on.

He shrugs, then reluctantly replaces the cigarette in his pack.

I lie back and pull out my brother's letter. I smooth it out, leaving a greasy smear of ointment and blood across the page.

Loony lies on his stomach, staring into the bush.

I pick up my pen.

We're somewhere in Quang Ngai province, heading for Son Ha. There's been reported movement of the 2nd VC regiment. We've been sent out to recon the area.

I don't know what the hell I'm doing here. I don't think Loony does either, and neither of us cares what the hell Charlie's doing. We just want to live through this.

It's ironic, but doing what we've been sent out here to do seems to be the best way to accomplish that.

I dreamed I was back in school. It seems to be the only way I can really imagine your world. When I'm awake, all that's real is what's here.

I was in my Asian History class. Dr. Miles was lecturing. I could see myself seated behind my desk, but I don't think the self I was seeing exists anymore. It's only been two years since I was on campus. But in real time, Nam time, it's more like a hundred years ago.

I remember I use to sit with the campus anarchists in the student union and talk about this war. But there's no longer any room for words in this world I'm in now. It's all unintelligible sound. The screech of Phantoms sweeping an area, the hollow whistle of incoming fire, and the screams of the survivors. All communication is reduced to noise, and what speaks the loudest is the most deadly.

I don't want you to come here. If they try to send you here, I want you to go to Canada. I've heard they're accepting war protesters. You don't belong here. No one...

Loony touches my leg. My pen jerks across the page. It leaves a ragged line of blue ink from top to bottom.

He moves beside me and pulls off his helmet, then places it beneath his head and lies back.

I put away the letter and take position.

The growth is thick and impenetrable. Vision is reduced to a three foot circumference.

I rest my chin along the stock of my 16. The metal is warm and feels strangely soothing.

I stare out at the bush and wait, wait to move, wait for Charlie, wait for it all to be over.

8

Nancy Helke lives at the end of our street. She has black hair that sits on her head like a bowl and blue eyes. No one in my family has blue eyes. My mother, John, and me all have brown eyes. My father has grey eyes. Nancy's eyes look like the pictures I've seen of the ocean where my grandfather lives.

She's standing by the apple tree in the field behind our house. It's the first time I've seen her anywhere but school. She's wearing white shorts and a grey sweater.

I lean against the trunk and look at her.

Nancy picks up an old wrinkled apple.

"I bet you I can throw this all the way out to the road."

"Bet you can't."

She heaves back her arm and throws. She doesn't throw like a girl.

She grins.

"You didn't hit the road."

"How do you know?"

"Cause we would have heard it."

"I heard it."

"I didn't."

"You weren't listening."

"Do it again."

"There aren't any more apples."

"Throw this." I hand her a rock.

When she throws, her hair whips across her forehead. Parts of it stick out from the top of her head.

"I can't tell where it went."

"You try."

I'm about to throw when she suddenly grabs my arm. "Shhhh," she hisses, then I hear the sound of a car.

We grin at each other and wait for the car to pass, then I throw.

"I didn't hear anything."

"Neither did I."

"You threw it hard. Maybe it went all the way across the road into Mr. Welty's flowers."

"I didn't throw it that hard."

She shrugs and walks over to the apple tree and sits. After a moment I join her. We talk about school. I tell her about Mrs. Sherwood, and how she should watch out for her. She tells me about Mr. Paul, who she says is her favorite teacher of all time.

I hear my mother call.

"I have to go eat now."

"Me, too. I'll see you tomorrow," she calls, and runs down the path.

When I come into the house, my mother asks why I'm smiling. I tell her I don't know.

As I'm washing my hands, I think the water looks just like the ocean.

We're having pork chops, apple sauce, and green beans. John and I have milk, my father has a gin and tonic, and my mother has water.

"Burdick thinks it bears watching," my father says.

"I can't believe it will come to anything. And even if it does, Senator Kennedy will make sure it's over quickly."

"You and your precious Mr. Kennedy," my father sneers.

"He's a good man."

My father puts a piece of pork chop in his mouth and starts to chew. "What are you looking at?"

I shift my glance to my plate. I can feel his eyes on me. They feel heavy.

"Jack, do you want another?"

My father turns away and nods.

My mother picks up the platter and walks around the table. When she stands beside him, my father touches the back of her leg.

John and I do the dishes. John washes and I dry. My mother and father are in the other room. We can hear the sound of my mother's laughter.

"She's happy."

John shrugs and hands me a plate.

"How come she's happy?"

"She likes him."

"She has to like him, they're married."

"Just because you're married doesn't mean you have to like someone."

"Why would you marry them then?"

"You don't know anything."

"Do too. I know lots of things."

"Like what?"

"Like..." I pause, trying to think of something I know. It's hard because John is grinning at me.

The pan slips out of my hand and clatters to the floor.

"What's going on out there!" my father shouts.

"Nothing, it was just a pan," John calls.

We wait for the sound of his footsteps. We hear my mother's voice, but can't hear the words.

When she stops talking, my father yells, "Well, god dammit, be careful."

"You almost got us in trouble."

"I didn't mean to do it."

"Nobody means anything," John says.

I dry the pan, waiting for him to explain, but he never does.

I climb into bed. John lies on the floor by the door.

"What're you doing?"

"Nothing," he whispers, and rests his chin on his hands.

I slide over to join him.

"What...."

"Shhh," he warns.

A thin strip of light shows beneath my parent's room. I hear the sound of someone breathing, then the squeak of wood and springs. The breathing grows louder. "Who's making that noise?" I giggle.

"Quiet, or else you'll get us in trouble."

I'm about to say something when I hear my mother's voice. She's moaning. "What's he doing to her?"

"It's okay."

"He's hurting her!"

"He hurts everybody," John says, and climbs into bed.

I hear my mother groan, then everything gets quiet.

"He killed her!"

John shakes his head and picks up his book.

"Are you sure?"

"I'm sure."

He won't look at me. I cock my head to the side and listen.

I climb into bed and lie awake, waiting to hear my mother's voice, afraid he really hurt her bad this time.

When I hear my parent's door open, I creep over to the doorway.

Footsteps pad across the floor, the bathroom door opens, closes.

I lie on my stomach. I feel my heart thudding against my hands.

The toilet flushes, then the bathroom door opens.

If my mother is dead, would we have to live with my father... all alone?

I stare into the darkness, feeling my eyes getting hot.

A shadow moves across the hall. It's too small to be my father. I smile, then freeze as the bedroom door opens.

For an instant my mother is standing in the hallway. The light from the bedroom splashes all around her. She is naked. I can see her back and thighs. And when she closes the door, I see a thick patch of dark hair between her legs.

I climb into bed, feeling sick and sweaty that I've seen her like that. I want to tell her I'm sorry, but it would only make her mad.

I lie in bed, whispering I'm sorry over and over again until I fall asleep.

I'm reading a book about a boy who is captured by Indians. The Indians take him to their camp and tie him to a post. One of the Indians wants to kill him. The boy is very afraid, but he knows his father will come and save him. He has just spotted his father hiding behind a tree, when Mrs. Sherwood says, "What do you think you are doing?"

"Nothing."

"What's this?" She grabs my book and looks at it. "You are supposed to be reading your history book now."

"I already read it."

"Oh you did, did you?" She grins. "Then why don't you tell me what year did Illinois become a state?"

"1818," I answer.

Mrs. Sherwood glares. "What two American presidents resided in Illinois?"

"Abraham Lincoln and Ulysses S. Grant."

"Who was the first governor of Illinois?"

"I don't know. That wasn't in the bo..."

"Well, you would know if you were doing what you were supposed to be doing."

"But it wasn't in..."

"One more word out of you, and you're going to the office. Do you understand?"

"Yes," I whisper.

"And since you seem to enjoy reading so much, why don't you read chapter six and seven for me and give me a two page book report by tomorrow."

Mrs. Sherwood smiles at the other students, then walks back to her desk.

I stare at her back, wondering why she hates me so much.

"You have to hate her as much as she hates you," John explains. We're in the boy's bathroom at the end of the hall.

"I do hate her."

"Not enough." He throws his arm around my shoulders. "It's okay, you only have her for the rest of the year."

"But I have to read two whole chapters and write a book report, and I didn't even do anything."

"Don't cry."

"I'm not going to cry." I sniffle.

"I'll help you."

"You will?"

"I said I would." John walks towards the door. I start to follow.

He turns to look at me.

I stop and wait for him to go. I count to twenty five before I leave the bathroom.

By the time I get out to the playground, he's on the other side with Johnny and Randy.

"I heard you have to write a book report." Bobby grins.

"Yeah, but my brother said he'd help."

"He won't help, he only said that so you wouldn't cry."

"I wasn't going to cry."

Bobby takes a step back. His smile widens. "Crybaby, crybaby," he starts to sing.

"Am not," I say, bunching my fists.

"Are too," Bobby yells.

I charge. Bobby runs. I chase him for the rest of recess.

When the bell rings, I catch sight of John. He sees me watching him. He glances at Johnny and Randy, then quickly nods and looks away.

Mrs. Sherwood glares at me when I take my seat. I smile back at her, thinking I'm going to hate her more than she can ever hate me.

9

We're about twenty klicks out, deep into the mountains, when Loony grabs my arm. I spin out of his grip and fall into a crouch. We're a couple yards off the side of a trail.

Loony's hand clamps around my neck. He turns my head and points to the trail ahead. I scan the bush, trying to dissect the shadows, trying to see what he sees. I spot a flicker of dark movement. My grip tightens around the shotgun. I feel the tight press of Loony's eyes on my back as I watch the shadows begin to take form.

There are two of them, twenty yards ahead, moving along each side of the path. They're each carrying M-14's. They move with a silence that is terrifying to witness.

Loony nudges my side.

I shrug him off.

He grips my shoulder insistently.

I shake my head and hold up a fist. He lowers his weapon. We watch Charlie move towards us.

In their loosely fitted black outfits, they seem strangely unthreatening. It's only as they grow closer, and I see their faces the danger becomes readily apparent.

Their eyes are in constant movement, shifting through the terrain, cataloging its contours.

Dead eyes searching for a target.

They pass within feet of where we're crouched. Neither of us turns to watch, afraid they'll pick up the intensity of our gaze.

We stay in position for another five minutes, then dropped back into the bush and wait.

This time we hear them before we see them. The soft rustle of clothes, the metallic click of weapons, the quiet shuffle of feet announces the arrival of the patrol. They move in single file.

We wait for them to pass, then give them another twenty minutes before we move out.

We climb up to a ledge and Loony sets up the PRC. I take a position which gives me a view of the mountain side. I search the area, knowing they're down there, but unable to spot them.

I hear Loony's hoarse whisper behind me, relaying our coordinates.

Forty minutes later, as we move into a shallow declivity, we hear the sound of artillery fire behind us.

Loony grins in satisfaction.

As the sun hangs in the western horizon, we come to rocky outcropping, commanding a view of each side of the slope.

I motion Loony forward. He stoops and slowly walks up to the rocks. He pauses three feet in front of a waist high boulder. He drops to his heels and studies the area. After a moment he carefully places his weapon behind him and eases forward.

I drop back and fall into a crouch.

Loony's hands float across the surface of the ground, gently probing. He pauses, runs his hand to one side, then the other.

He draws a wavering line in the dirt, then hunches forward and steps over the scrawled configuration.

He draw four more lines across the ground before he disappears behind one of the boulders.

I brush away a line of red ants climbing up my boot. The sun flashes brightly then ducks behind one of the western peaks. The sweat begins to cool along my back and shoulders. I shiver, then wave at a cloud of mosquitoes circling my face, darting at my eyes and nose.

Loony appears among the rocks.

He holds up six fingers, then holds his hands out, palm down and shakes them.

I nod and start to move.

As I come to the first line in the dirt, I can just make out the trip wire running to each side. I step over it, then turn and carefully erase Loony's marking. I move forward, circumventing each of the lines, then wipe them away.

Behind the first outcropping, Loony had placed six coin sized rocks in the dirt, in no apparent design.

He makes a fist, raises it in the air, then abruptly spreads his fingers.

Bettys, I think, looking at the rocks, remembering Dexter and the hot taste of his blood as it splattered across my face.

Our position is solid. Rocks to three sides of us, mountains behind. The only access is through the mine field.

I dump my pack and lean against a boulder, then slide to the ground. I pull up my legs and crouch forward, resting my arms on my knees.

Loony's cupped hand appears in my line of vision.

I hit the cigarette greedily and pull the smoke into my lungs.

Loony hits it once more, then carefully stubs it out and buries the butt.

He catches my eye, shrugs, then shakes his head wearily.

His face is stained with dirt and sweat. His neck and cheeks are pebbled with insect bites. His eyes are cavernous and seemingly huge.

He pulls a groundsheet from his pack and spreads it across the dirt. He lies on his back, his head on his helmet, and stares at the sky.

I hang forward in the cavern between my legs. I think about the letter to my brother, but can't summon the energy to dig it out of my pack. And even if I could, what would I write?

How could I explain this?

How can I explain anything anymore?

I watch Loony sleep, envying him, then rise and move to the rocks. I look out at the rolling hills, washing into sharp, jutting ridges, trying to remember what it is I'm supposed to be looking for.

What is it I'm supposed to be doing out here?

Enemy movement.

The enemy moves. We all know the enemy moves. What we don't know is how to stop him, or even where he is moving to.

We know nothing about him, except he bleeds the same way we do, his screams are the same as ours, and he kills with a deadly efficiency we can't seem to emulate.

I lean back and try to pull off my boots. My feet are too swollen. I'll have to cut them off when I get back to base.

The only way they'll ever heal is if I can dry them out, and the only way to dry them out is to take off my boots... but they won't come off.

I stagger to Loony's side and collapse on the edge of his groundsheet. A cloud of mosquitoes moves in front of me. I grab my pack and dig out the bug juice and smear it over my hands and face.

Loony's cheeks and forehead are covered with mosquitoes. I waved them away and pour juice on his face. He groans, shakes his head, sleeps.

A wave of nausea drives me to the ground. I lie on my back. The sky is dark and studded with cold stars. The drone of insects trying to penetrate my flesh follows me as I fall into a restless sleep.

10

Bobby tells me his father killed people in the war.

"How do you know?"

"Cause he told me."

"How many people did he kill?"

"Lots of them," Bobby says. "He was a hero."

Bobby runs into the field. I follow, shooting at all the Koreans trying to catch us.

"Was Daddy in the war?"

"No, your father was too old."

"How old was he?"

"Too old."

John and I are on the couch on each side of my mother watching TV.

"Mr. Shore was in the war."

My mother nods and turns away.

"Did daddy want to be in the war?"

"Why do you keep asking me about this?"

"I don't know."

John rolls his eyes and shakes his head.

"Your father tried to enlist but he was too old, that's all there was to it."

"But he wanted to go to war, didn't he?"

"Yes, he wanted to go. Now lets not talk about this anymore."

I smile and turned to the TV. I feel my mother looking at me. When I turn to see why, she shakes her head and looks away.

"Was your father in the war?"

"I don't know." Nancy shrugs. "Was yours?"

"No, but he wanted to go."

Nancy points to a branch above us. "Look, there's a praying mantis."

We climb the tree to look at it. Nancy breaks off a branch and pokes it in the side. The insect falls to the ground.

Nancy leans over to look, as she starts to sit back up her hand slips.

I catch her by the arm. Her skin feels different than John or Bobby's. I suddenly remember the sight of my mother standing in the hallway, the dark hair between her legs. I wonder if Nancy has hair like that, too.

"You saved my life."

"Would you save my life if I was falling?"

"Of course, stupid, who wouldn't?"

"I bet old Mrs. Sherwood wouldn't. I bet she'd just let me fall right on my head."

"Lets go higher."

Before I can answer, she starts to climb. She's wearing blue shorts and a white shirt.

I look up to see her moving to a higher branch. Her shorts rise over her legs. I see the white edge of her underwear.

"C'mon, climb up here."

I stand on my toes to reach for a branch. Before I can hoist myself up I hear a cracking sound. I look up to see Nancy falling down at me.

I try to grab her but she falls too fast.

She hits the branch I'm standing on, then bounces all the way to the ground.

She moans then curls up on her side.

I scramble down the tree and kneel beside her.

Her shoulders hitch. Her arms tighten around her knees.

"Are you all right?" I touch her back.

When I touch her, she sobs.

"Do you want me to get your mother?"

She shakes her head.

"Where does it hurt?"

She starts to cry more loudly.

I don't know what to do.

Nancy reaches for me. I take her hand, thinking I'll help her up, but she pulls me to the ground. She won't let go of me.

I hold her while she cries.

After I while I start to pat her back. I say, "It's okay," over and over again, the way my mother does to me.

Nancy limps beside me as we walk towards her house. It's late. I know I'm going to get in trouble when I get home, but I'm afraid if I leave her she'll die. Her face is streaked with dirt and tears. The side of her shirt is ripped and hangs out from her shorts. Her knee is still bleeding.

"You don't think I'll have to get stitches, do you?" Her voice is shaky.

"It's not so bad." I smile to let her know I mean it.

As we come to her house, her father walks out to the road.

"Daddy!" Nancy wails, and runs to him.

He rushes to her and wraps his arms around her. Nancy buries her face into the side of his neck and cries.

Mr. Helke's eyes bite into me.

"What have you done!"

I shake my head and back away. "I didn't do anything."

"Get over here," he yells. "Right now!"

I keep backing away.

"What did you do to my little girl?" Mr. Helke starts down the road towards me.

I turn and run. I hear him shouting, but I keep running.

The lights are on in the dining room. I creep around the side of the house and peek inside. Everyone is at the dinner table. John is staring at his plate. My mother keeps glancing towards the door. My father's eyes are hard.

Feeling the heat building behind my eyes, I walk to the back door and open it as quietly as I can.

"Where the hell have you been!" my father yells. I hear his footsteps coming down the hall.

I whimper and whirl around, trying to find some place to hide.

"Do you know what the hell time it is!"

"Jack," my mother calls from the dining room.

"God dammit, how many time have I've told you." His lips are thin. His eyes look like bullets.

"Where the hell were you." He slaps me across the face. I fall against the wall.

"I didn't do anything," I tell him, trying not to cry. I know it only makes him madder.

"Where were you??" His hands are on his hips. His eyes are eating my face. He slaps me again.

"Jack, please, don't," my mother says from the hallway.

He glares at her then turns on me.

"Well, mister, just where the hell have you been all night."

"I was just at the…"

"Don't you dare lie to me." He raises his hand.

I flinch and try to duck away.

He grabs my shoulder and twists me around. His hand slashes across my cheek.

His eyes bore into me, pinning me in place. I can't move. I'm afraid if I move, or if I even I talk he'll hit me again.

"I'm waiting. Where the hell were you?"

"I was by the apple tree. I was with…"

"God dammit! You were not by the apple tree. We looked. Now don't you dare lie to me again," he shouts, and crouches until he's right in my face. He grabs my shoulders and shakes me.

John appears in the doorway. He looks at my mother, my father, then back at me. His face is very white.

"Don't you dare look at your brother when I'm talking to you." He raises his hand. I cower against the door. He slaps me across the ear. Everything goes dark. I fall against the wall.

He grabs me by the shoulders and hits me again.

His lips are moving but I can't hear. I can only see my mother backing out of the room. I look for John, but he's gone too. It's only me and my father... my father's eyes.

He hits me again, then keeps hitting me.

I want to tell him I can't hear, but I know he'll think I'm lying, because I always lie to him.

My mother appears at the door.

My father looks at her.

Her lips move.

My father listens, after a moment he nods, then turns to me.

I flinch and try to hide.

He shakes his head, says something, then leaves the room.

I slide to the floor. I can't hear myself crying, but I can feel my mother's arms close around me. She helps me to my feet and up the stairs. She sits on edge of my bed and pats my back. I fall asleep while she's there.

When I wake, she's gone, but it's all right because I can hear again. I listen to the silence of the house, the sound of my brother's breathing until I fall asleep.

11

When we're not climbing, we're fighting our way through thick stands of bamboo. The stalks tower above our heads and slice through our palms. The heat sucks the moisture from our bodies. The lands shifts, twists, drops, then rises again. We stagger forward, exhausted, unable to see ten feet ahead.

We break behind some rocks. Loony lights a cigarette. I watch, unable to find the energy to stop him.

"Where the fuck are we?"

I shake my head and look at the map between my knees. I know we're in the mountains somewhere outside Son Ha, but I'm not sure where.

We've been traveling for thirty six hours without finding any signs of Charlie. All the movement we've discovered so far, appears to be concentrated to the north and to the east.

Our destination on the aerials is highlighted by a peak. I trace its curve as it shifts and winds its way up into a constantly gathering ridge of mountains.

I rise unsteadily and lean against the rocks as I try to get a visual fix on our location. Loony sits with his head hanging between his knees. His weapon lies across his lap.

I scan the area until I find a corresponding silhouette. I memorize its shape, then return to the map.

"I got it."

"Big fucking deal," Loony mutters, without lifting his head.

"About five more klicks."

"Then we can go home?"

"Yeah." I nod. "Then we can go home."

We sit, trying to gather our strength, then push to our feet and start climbing again.

I'm too tired to think. I move forward because it's all I can do. Any other option would take too much thought.

A flash of green slithers through the bush around my boots. I keep moving.

I feel something tear on my left foot, then feel a spurt of hot moisture leaking across my instep.

A wave of gnats and flies hovers around my face. They dart at my eyes and ears.

I spot a trail of black dots along the inside of my wrist. I brush the ants away. One of them splits in half. Its jaws keep moving, keeps chewing its way into my flesh.

The sun centers above us. It sends piercing shafts of light along the stalks until it rivets us to the damp earth.

I stumble and fall to my knees. My breath rasps hoarsely through my throat.

Loony looks back at me. His chest heaves as he struggles to pull in enough air.

I use my weapon to lever myself up. I wobble, lock my knees in place, then stagger forward.

Loony falls in behind.

The elephant grass begins to thin. The ground grows rockier.

A hill looms in front of us. It slopes upward, then abruptly grows steeper as it rises and falls, always ascending, climbing to its peak, our destination.

We sweep the area, then break inside a cluster of boulders. The rocks give us a clean position up and down. Everything to either side is impassable.

Loony pulls a cigarette. The scent of the smoke wafts over to me. I cling to my canteen, trying to find the energy to lift it to my mouth.

Loony grins loosely, nods, then slowly slumps against the rocks. His cigarette is still burning between his fingers.

Groaning, I crawl over and kill the butt. I wobble back to the rocks and fall against them. A swarm of gnats move towards my eyes. I blink...

The noise wakes me. It's a child's voice. I laze against the rock in the baking sun, still half asleep, listening to the song. It's a tuneless effort that seems to go on endlessly.

It's only as I focus on Loony seated across from me that I remember where I am.

I lunge for my weapon.

The sound is coming from above. Adrenalin surges through me, wiping away the last vestiges of sleep.

I scramble to Loony's side and nudge him. I clamp a hand over his mouth as he starts to speak. His eyes find mine and grow large as he hears the child's voice.

I shake my head and release him.

I move into the rocks and scan the ridge above. The voice fades. Loony comes up beside me. His gaze is waiting for mine.

"I don't know," I whisper.

He points towards the ridge.

We move out and begin to climb. My movements are sure and coordinated. The pain and exhaustion are gone. All that remains is the fear, and the tight wire of adrenalin running through me.

"What the fuck is that?" Loony mutters bewilderedly.

I shake my head. I have no answer.

We've taken position on the edge of a plateau, a hundred yards below the peak. The plateau is no more than fifty by thirty yards long and wide. It backs up against a steep, rocky incline. The front of it ends at a ledge overlooking the valley.

A hut has been erected against the rock. Its walls are made of bamboo. The pitched roof is covered with tightly bound sheaths of grass. To the side is a small bamboo pen. Two pigs wallow in the mud.

The dirt surrounding the hut is tightly packed and bare of any foliage. The child's singing is coming from inside the hooch.

Loony holds up one finger and looks at me for confirmation.

I don't have an answer. I continue studying the front of the hut, trying to see into the dark entrance.

A thin stream of smoke drifts up through the roof. It smells greasy and foreign.

Loony nudges my shoulder. He gestures to his right, then motions to the other side.

I hold up both hands, fixing him in place.

We wait and watch, trying to decide whether to move around, or through the area.

Our orders are ambiguous and open to interpretation. Recon the area, avoid all enemy contact, unless an opportunity for further information is available.

The child continues singing.

Loony nudges me more insistently.

I nod. We start to move.

I ease into the clearing, slithering along the ground. The sun presses on my back and legs. The earth smells rich and fertile. My hand closes around a rock. Its shape impresses itself into every pore of my palm. The faint odor of gun oil and sweat fills my nostrils. It all blends together in a trenchantly vivid panorama that terrifies me.

The child's voice suddenly halts. I freeze. The silence crashes into me and thuds through my head.

A parrot's screech pierces the silence.

I see a shape begin to take form in the dark interior of the hut.

I level my weapon.

I watch as the shadow slowly begins to reveal itself.

Bare feet move into the sunlight. Legs, torn white pants, a dark rag tied around the waist, faded green t-shirt, flash of light at the neck.

Dog tags!

I leap to my feet and start moving. Loony comes up on my flank. Our weapons are trained on the figure in front of the hooch.

A man stands in the sunlight, smiling at us. He raises his hands in greeting.

"Who the fuck are you?" Loony gasps.

I can't take my eyes from the man's smile, the ironic twist of his lips, welcoming us, gesturing us in to join him.

12

Our garage has a concrete floor and wooden walls with holes in them. The walls aren't painted and are covered with spider webs. There is no room in the garage for my father's car so he parks outside. He only goes in the garage on week-ends to get his hammer or his fishing pole. One time, after he got in a fight with my mother, I saw my father go into the garage on a Tuesday. I ran over to the window to see what he was going to do. By the time I got to the window, he'd already opened his fishing box and pulled out a small brown bottle. He sat on a wooden chest and drank.

When he was done he put the bottle back in his tackle box and went into the house. I waited until he was inside before I snuck into the garage.

The bottle had a picture of big red crow on the front of it. It tasted like medicine. It made my stomach burn.

The only time I ever saw my brother cry was when I hit him in the head with a baseball bat. I was up at bat and John was catching. Terry was pitching. He kept calling me names when he threw the ball.

"Don't listen to him," John whispered. "He's just trying to make you mad so you'll miss. Take your time."

I waited for the next pitch, then swung as hard as I could. I felt the bat smash into something, then watched the ball roll to the ground in front of me. I turned when I heard the noise behind me.

John was standing straight up. He had both of his hands pressed to the side of his head. His mouth was bleeding.

"John?"

He staggered and fell to the ground. Before I could move, Terry pushed me out of the way and rushed to John's side.

"Is he dead?"

"Go get your mother!" Terry yelled.

I started to run. I heard John crying behind me.

"I killed John!" I wailed, as I burst into the house.

"What!"

"I didn't mean to. It was an accident. I hit him with the baseball bat, and he's going to..."

My mother grabbed me by the arms and shook me. "Where is he?"

"He's at Terry's. It was an acc..."

But she was already out the door.

I waited in the driveway. I was too afraid to go back to Terry's. I wondered what my father would do to me.

"I didn't mean it," I whispered, and started to cry.

My mother came running down the street. She was carrying John. He had his arms around her neck, and there was blood all over the front of her shirt. He was still crying.

"Go call Mrs. Shore, tell her we need a ride to the doctor's!" she yelled.

I couldn't move, all I could hear was John crying.

"Hurry dammit!" my mother shouted.

"It's okay, baby," she said to John, and touched his hair with her chin.

John got four stitches in his lip. He had pieces of string in his mouth for one whole week. He said it was okay I hit him with the baseball bat. He knew I hadn't mean to do it.

"She picked you up and carried you all the way home."

"It hurt a lot," John said, touching his lip.

"She carried you home,' I whispered.

That night I dreamed I was the one who got hit with the baseball bat, and my mother was carrying me. Her arms were wrapped around me so tightly, my head didn't hurt at all.

"He thought you hurt me," Nancy says. I'm teaching her how to catch crayfish.

"Why'd he think that?"

"I don't know." She's wearing blue shorts and pink shirt today. She has a band-aid on her knee.

"Does it still hurt?"

"Not too much. Do you want to see it?"

"Nah," I say, then point to the water. "See that brick?"

Nancy leans forward and nods.

"You have to watch real close, because they're very fast."

I flip over the brick. A puff of mud floats to the surface, then slowly drifts away.

"I see it!" Nancy yells. "It's right there."

I ease my hand behind the crayfish's back, then grab it. When I pull it out, Nancy backs away.

"Don't be afraid, it can't get you."

She makes a face, then moves closer. "Will it bite me?"

"They don't bite, they pinch," I say, then show her how to hold it.

We carry it to the side of the summer house and sit down.

"You try it now." I put it on the grass between us. "Just pick it up like I showed you."

Nancy lowers her hand behind the crayfish. It suddenly darts backwards. She squeals and jerks away.

"It tried to bite me."

"They don't bite, they pinch," I tell her again.

She makes a face and asks me again to show her how to hold it. She leans over to watch. I feel her breath on the side of my face.

"Okay, it's your turn." I put the crayfish on the grass. "Now don't..."

Before I can finish, she picks it up. She holds it in the air and laughs. The crayfish's tail flaps back and forth and its pincers open and close.

Nancy giggles, then jabs it at me.

I bob out of the way.

She laughs and follows.

"Don't," I tell her, but I'm smiling.

She grins and shoves the crayfish at me.

I grab her legs and pull her to the ground. She rolls to her side and throws the crayfish at me. It hits my chest and falls into the grass.

"I got you!" she yells.

"I got you!" I shout, and jump on her. We roll down the hill towards the lake. Her arms wrap around my back, pushing and pulling me.

When we stop rolling, I'm on top. I grab her arms. She fights. I put her arms beneath each of my knees and pin her to the ground.

She tries to kick, but I shift out of the way.

"Let me up."

"Not until you give."

"Im not going to give."

"Then I'm not going to let you up."

"Oh, yes you will," she says, then suddenly twists to the side. Her knee pumps into my back. Before I can catch myself, she wiggles away then grabs my shoulders and throws herself on me. I fall back and she lands on top of me. Our breath rasps in our throats as we wrestle for control.

She lunges forward until she's sitting on my chest. She has both of my hands in hers and is trying to pin me to the ground. I don't try as hard as I can because she's girl.

She shifts forward, struggling to hold me in place. Her face is only inches from mine.

"I got you now," she gasps.

"Oh, no you don't."

"Oh, yes I do." She grins, then suddenly leans over and kisses me right on the mouth.

I'm so surprised I stop fighting.

She swivels around and pins both of my hands beneath her knees.

"Give?"

"That wasn't fair."

"You're bigger than I am."

"But you still can't cheat."

"How did I cheat?"

"You..." I stop. She's smiling at me.

"What?"

I hunch forward and throw her off. She rolls to the side and lies on her stomach. "Are you mad?"

"Why would I be mad?"

"Because I kissed you."

I look around to make sure no one heard her.

"That's what girls and boys do," she says, then walks down to the pier. She sits on the edge and dangles her feet over the water.

"Do what?" I sit beside her.

"They kiss." Nancy giggles. She covers her mouth with her hands.

"Grownups do that."

"Not just grownups. I saw Barry Miller and Joyce doing it."

"They're in high school."

"They do more than kiss," she says quietly.

"What do you mean?"

"They do other stuff, too."

"What kind of stuff?"

"Stuff that adults do."

"Like what?"

Nancy looks at me for a moment, then leans over until her face is right next to mine. "Do you want me to show you?"

She's so close I'm afraid she's going to kiss me again. I pull back. "Who cares what Barry and Joyce do." I peel away a splinter from the edge of the pier.

"They're stupid." Nancy agrees.

I throw the splinter into the water and watch it float away.

"My father said he's going to buy a boat this summer."

"My father already has a boat. You want to see it? It's right over there." I point to the other side of Mr. Welty's yard.

"Can we go out in it?"

"Only my father gets to go out in it."

"Let's go look at it." Nancy starts up the hill.

"It's faster if we go across Mr. Welty's yard."

"We'll get in trouble."

"Not if we run real fast."

"What if Mr. Welty sees us?"

"He won't see us."

She shakes her head and starts up the hill.

"I dare you!"

She stops and looks back at me.

"I double dare you!" I shout.

Nancy clenches her teeth, then suddenly whirls and starts to run towards Mr. Welty's yard.

I take off after her. Her legs flash in front of me. As I'm about to catch up to her, I slow down and let her beat me.

She stops on the other side of the property.

"Beat you," she grins.

I take her to my father's boat. I sit in the front and she sits in back. I pretend we're rowing far out into the lake, just the two of us, where no will yell at us, or think I'm doing something bad to her.

13

"How you doing?" The man smiles amiably. "I'm Lester, that's Hoang."

I tear my eyes from the man and glance over at the hut. A small boy is standing in the entrance way. He rocks back and forth as he sings.

"Who the fuck are you?" Loony asks incredulously.

"Nobody special." The man shrugs and turns to smile at Loony.

Loony and I are a few feet to either side of him. Our weapons are trained at the ground in front of his feet.

The man's skin has an almost translucent quality. Dark veins run thickly across his forehead. He is wearing an old, tattered army fatigue t-shirt. His white pants are stained and torn and end a good six inches above his ankles.

"You must be hungry." The man turns to the boy. "Hoang." He gestures to his mouth, then points to us.

Still singing, the boy darts into the hut.

Loony slides over to the hooch. His weapon is leveled at the door.

The man, Lester, watches Loony with a bemused expression on his pale features.

He is very tall and exceedingly thin. His jaw juts out sharply from the sunken hollows of his cheeks, which make the ironic twist of his lips all the more incongruous.

"What the fuck is going on here?" Loony whispers.

I shrug and look to the man for an explanation.

"It is rather hot, isn't it." He motions to the side of the hooch.

I follow him into the shade. He lowers himself to his heels. His lanky body folds neatly around itself.

The boy steps out of the hooch carrying two bowls. Humming tunelessly, he hands a bowl to Loony, then walks over to me. His eyes glitter darkly as he offers me the food. Searching his gaze, I see only my own reflection.

"Hoang has had a difficult time," the man says. He raises his arm. The boy ducks beneath it and burrows against his side. The boy's eyes follow our every move.

"Who are you?"

"Eat, you must be hungry. I've been watching you for some time now."

"What the hell are you talking about?" Loony moves into the shadows, his weapon remains pointed at the man's feet.

"Down there." The man waves to the edge of the plateau. "I spotted you a couple of days ago." He smiles, shakes his head. "I thought for sure you were going to walk right into that patrol." He nods admiringly. "You did very well for yourselves." He digs a finger into the boy's ear. The boy giggles.

"Shit!" Loony explodes. "Who the fuck are you, and what the fuck are you doing here?"

The man slowly turns to face Loony, only his head moves, his body stays perfectly still. "I'm Lester," he says calmly. "And I live here. What are you doing here?"

Loony glares at him.

"Where are we?" I ask.

"A little outside of Son Ha."

"How far outside?"

"Mile or so that way." He motions to the east.

"A mile," I say, softly emphasizing the word.

"Yes." He smiles knowingly. "A mile."

"Take a look.' I motion Loony into the hut. He throws his bowl to the ground and edges through the doorway.

The boy begins to sing.

"I was wondering how long you were planning on staying." He smiles disarmingly. "I hadn't really figured on guests, so we're not very well prepared for visitors."

"That's all right," I say absently, concentrating on Loony's movements inside the hut.

"Good, I'd hate to disappoint."

"Nothing," Loony reports, stepping through the doorway.

"Weapons?"

"No."

I turn to the man. "Where's the woman?"

"What woman?"

"His mother." I nod to Hoang.

"He has no mother. He has only me."

"And who are you again?"

"I'm his father." The man rises to his feet and moves towards me. "I'm Lester."

Loony raises his weapon.

Lester pauses in front of me with his hand extended.

I study his face, trying to read something in his features, then grip his hand and introduce myself.

"And you must be Loony," the man says, turning away from me. "I've heard so much about you."

Loony reluctantly accepts the hand. His bewildered gaze finds mine.

I turn away from the silent question. I have no answers. The boy's glance catches my eye, his dark stare centers me.

"This is bullshit, man. What the fuck are we doing here?"

We've moved around to the other side of the hut. Lester and the boy are inside, preparing more food.

"I don't know."

"Then why don't we just get out of here. This guy's out of his fucking mind."

"What's he doing out here?"

"Who the hell cares what he's doing. Lets just get the fuck out while we can."

"He's one of ours."

"So what?"

"So we can't just leave him here."

"Why not?" He rushes on before I can reply. "The guy looks like he's been here for a while. He's doing okay. We should be worrying about our own asses, rather than some fucked up maniac living on the side of a mountain with some retard."

I try to find the words to fit my thoughts.

"It's not right," I conclude.

"What the fuck you mean, it's not right. We got to start worrying about what's not right now, too?"

"He's wearing tags. He's one of ours." I shake my head, then catch Loony's eye and add, "He just quit."

"Quit what?" Loony asks in frustration.

"The war."

"Oh shit," Loony moans.

"It's not fair," I say, turning to look at the valley below.

We eat rice and some kind of meat wrapped in dark steamed leaves.

"Monkey," Lester explains, when Loony asks him about the meat.

Loony snorts in disgust and pulls a cigarette.

"May I have one of those, please."

Loony shakes one out then lights them both up.

Lester leans against the wall of the hut and smokes, looking thoughtfully at the horizon. The shadows are just beginning climb up our legs.

The boy lies on the ground beside Lester, drawing in the dirt with a stick.

"It'll be a nice sunset tonight." Lester nods to the distant ridge.

"Right," Loony says sarcastically.

I push my bowl aside and rise. "We need to set a perimeter. Up there, and down along there." I point to the path we took to the plateau.

Loony opens his pack and pulls out the claymores.

"No."

We both turn to look at Lester.

"There's no need for any of that."

"That's not the way we see it," I tell him, and motion to Loony to start.

"You don't understand," Lester says softly.

I ignore him and start up the trail, leading to the peak.

Twenty yards up, I lay a line of claymores.

When I return to the clearing, Lester and the boy are seated on the ground. Loony's a few feet in front of them, smoking and watching them curiously. He glances at me, nods, then goes back to his examination.

I step into the hut and look around. Hanging against one wall, from a bamboo rod, is a religious portrait of the crucifixion of Christ. Glowering over the top of the cross, is an image of God. The painted God's eyes seem glazed with rage, and his glance is not focused outward, but at the crucified Christ.

When I come outside, the boy and Lester are at the edge of the plateau. Lester is pointing something out to the boy. Loony's gaze is fixed on their backs.

As I moved to his side, I glance down and stop. I nudge Loony with my foot and point.

"Aw shit," Loony mutters as he looks at the ground.

They are four stick figures drawn in the dirt. Two of the figures are carrying weapons. The third is that of a child. Each of the stick figures is missing a limb. The fourth figure, drawn abnormally tall, towers over the other three. This figure is holding a head in his hands. The decapitated head is smiling, while the other three are crying, weeping pebble tears.

Lester walks over to us. The boy clings to his side.

I scrape my boot across the drawing.

"Good night," Lester says. "Sleep well." He smiles at both of us, then ducks into the hut. The boy begins to sing.

Loony looks at me.

I shrug and walk over to my pack. I pull out a groundsheet and spread it beside the edge of the hut.

"We're going to fucking stay here!" Loony asks incredulously.

I lie down and curl on my side. I wrap my arms around my knees.

"We shouldn't do this, man," Loony whispers. "It's too fucking wrong."

I close my eyes and listen to the boy's song.

14

Mr. and Mrs. Platt are coming to our house for dinner. Mr. Platt works with my father at his office. The grownups eat in the dining room while John and I have to eat in the kitchen. I like eating in the kitchen, it's safer, but it makes John mad. He thinks he's old enough to eat with the grownups.

"Nancy fell out of the apple tree."

"So what." He's still mad he can't eat in the other room.

"So her leg got all scraped up. She almost had to get stitches."

"Almost doesn't count."

"Only in hand grenades." I grin. I'm not sure what that means, but John always says it to me, and I know it's a joke.

"Hand grenades and horse shoes," John sneers.

I go back to cutting my steak. It's not a whole steak It's just a part of one. John has the other part. His looks bigger than mine, but I don't say anything.

From the dining room, I hear my father ask if anyone wants another drink. My mother and Mrs. Platt start laughing.

"She sounds happy."

John rolls his eyes.

"How come she's happy?"

"Just eat, and leave me alone."

John finishes first and carries his plate over to the sink.

"Mom, can I go out for a while?"

"Did you finish everything?"

"Yes."

"All right, but be back before dark."

Still chewing, I rush to the sink with my plate.

"Can I go, too?"

"All right."

"Where we going?" I ask.

"You're not coming with me. I'm going over to Terry's." Johns starts towards the door.

"Terry's not home. He had to go to J.A. tonight."

"When did you hear that?"

"On the bus."

"Boy, you sure have big ears." John snorts then opens the door. I follow him outside.

"Go ahead, it won't hurt you." John nudges me with his shoulder.

We're sitting beneath the picnic table. John is holding out the glass shaker my father and Mr. Platt left outside. There's still some martini left in the jug.   "What's it taste like?" It smells like berries and rubbing alcohol.

"It's kind of like medicine."

I hold my breath and take a sip. It burns and tastes sweet at the same time.

"What do you think?"

"It's not too bad."

John grins and reaches for the shaker. We finish the martini and run out to the apple tree. We each take a branch and sit with our legs swinging below us.

"Is this where Nancy fell?" John asks, then starts to laugh.

"It's not funny. She could have died," I say, then start laughing too. I don't know why I'm laughing.

"Did she fall on her head."

"On her knee. She bounced on this branch." I point to a branch below us. John laughs even harder.

I suddenly stop laughing. I want to get down. I start to move along the branch, then stop. I remember the way Nancy looked curled up on the ground.

"I bet she cried," John says, then turns to stare across the field at our house. "Girls always cry."

"John, I'm stuck."

He shakes his head then stands and starts to walk along the branch. He has to step around me. I close my eyes and hold my breath.

When I open them, he's holding on to the trunk of the tree. "You're not stuck. Just reach over there." He points to a branch.

"I can't. I'm scared."

"What're you scared of?"

"Everything," I moan, then start to cry.

"C'mon, don't cry. It's going to be all right."

"I don't want to die."

"You're not going to die. Just grab that branch."

"Nancy almost died."

"No, she didn't. She just hurt her knee."

"But she could have died."

John edges along the branch and sits beside me. I throw my arms around his waist. My fingers dig into his hip.

"It's going to be okay. Just follow me. I won't let anything happen to you." He puts his arm around my shoulders and slowly shifts sideways. Still sniffling I press against him.

We slide over to the tree trunk. "Now put your arm around it." He pries my fingers from his hip and moves them to the tree.

"How come you're so scared. You've done this before?"

I shake my head. The ground seems very far away.

John slides down to the next branch. "Now put your foot in my hand."

"I can't."

"Do it, or else I'm going to leave you here."

"Don't leave me!"

"Then put your foot in my hand."

I kick out and John grabs my foot. He guides it to the branch. "Now stand up. C'mon, you can do it. You're a big boy."

Whimpering, I slowly rise.

"See, you're doing good."

John leads me down the tree.

Once I get to the bottom I sit on the ground and look up. It doesn't seem that high anymore.

"Please, don't tell anybody what happened."

"I won't tell anyone." He grips my shoulder lightly. "We'd better get back, it's getting dark. "C'mon, I'll race you," he shouts, and takes off running.

"That's not fair, you got a head start," I yell, then charge after him, running to catch up.

I tell Nancy how Mrs. Welty died of cancer.

"Did it hurt?"

"It hurt a whole lot."

"How do you know?"

"I saw a book about it."

Nancy is lying on the ground in front of me. She's wearing blue jeans and a brown shirt.

"I'm not going to get cancer."

"How do you know?"

"Because I'm very healthy. That's what my doctor told me. He said I was a very healthy young woman."

"You're not a woman."

"I will be."

"Not for a long time."

"Only five years, and then I'll be a woman."

"You'll be," I pause to add up the numbers. "Thirteen. You'll be older than John."

"You'll be thirteen, too."

"Thirteen and six months."

Nancy makes a face and picks up a twig. She jabs it into the ground.

"In five years, John will be fifteen years old."

"So?" she shrugs.

"He'll be old."

Nancy looks at me, then smiles and says, "He'll still be your brother. He's always going to be your brother."

"Even if he doesn't want to." I grin.

"I almost had a brother, but he died before I was born."

"What was his name?"

"Edward."

"What happened to him?"

"My mother won't tell me. She just said he died and went to heaven."

"My grandmother went to heaven."

"Everyone goes to heaven."

"Not Mrs. Sherwood. I bet old Mrs. Sherwood will go to hell."

"You're not supposed to say that?"

"How come?"

"Because it's bad."

"Why's it bad?"

"I don't know. It just is." Nancy stands up and brushes off the front of her shirt. "Let's go down by the boat."

"I don't want to."

"What do you want to do?"

"I don't know. What do you want to do?"

"We could go to my house. My mother just made cookies."

"What kind?"

"Peanut butter."

"I don't like peanut butter cookies."

"You don't like my mother, do you?"

"I like your mother."

"Then how come you never want to come over to my house?"

I look away, trying to think of an answer.

"How come you don't like her?" she asks again, then kneels in front of me until there's no where else for me to look.

"Because."

"Because why?"

"Because she doesn't like me." I grab a handful of dirt and squeeze it.

"They're not mad at you anymore."

"I didn't do anything."

"I know. I told them," she says, then touches my shoulder. "They like you now."

"Really?"

"Honest." She grins and pulls on my shirt. "C'mon, lets go get some cookies."

"You sure she likes me?"

"Positive."

We run down the path to the road. I run just fast enough to keep along side of her.

Mrs. Helke gives us each two cookies and a glass of milk. She even smiles at me when she hands me my glass.

I thank her and we carry our milk and cookies out to the back porch.

Before I can take a bite, Mrs. Helke opens the door behind us. I turn to see her looking at me. I want to run, but I'm holding the glass of milk in my hand. I grit my teeth and wait for her to yell at me.

"I want to thank you, young man, for what you did for my daughter the other day. That was very brave and loyal of you." She smiles, then reaches to squeeze my shoulder. "You're welcome in our home any time you wish."

I blush and mumble a thank you.

Mrs. Helke turns and step inside the house.

"See," Nancy grins. "I told you."

15

I dream I'm standing over my father's grave again. My mother is beside me, on the other side of her is my brother. My mother is crying. When I turn to look at her, I catch my brother's eye. He smiles. I smile back. I hear a dog begin to howl.

I wake to see Loony kneeling beside me.
I run a hand over my eyes. The morning sun is blinding.
"You better take a look at this," he says uneasily.
My feet feel swollen and painful. I stumble, then regain my balance and follow him to the back of the hut.
"Where's the guy?"
He motions towards the peak.
"Why the hell did you let him go up there? We've got a line..."
Loony shakes his head and points to the ground.
Neatly stacked behind the hooch are all the claymores we laid out the night before.
"How the hell did that happen?" I mutter, staring at the mines, trying to comprehend how they could have been moved. It would take an incredible amount of skill, knowledge, and guts to disarm, then move the mines.

"Guy must've done it sometime last night." Loony pulls two cigarettes. "I found them here this morning."

"How'd he get out of the hut?"

"He must've walked right over us," he says, shaking his head in disbelief.

"You stay here. I'm going to go talk to him."

I find Lester sitting on a ledge overlooking the valley. His legs are bent and twisted so that his feet rest on each opposing thigh. His hands are lying in his lap palm upward. The kid is sitting beside him.

"Good morning," he says, without turning. "Did you sleep well?"

I crouch beside him.

He turns to me. His eyes crawl across my face.

"Any dreams?" he asks, with a knowing smile.

The smile irritates me. "You moved the claymores."

"I told you they weren't necessary. No one bothers us here."

"They may not bother you, but they've been bothering us."

"Then maybe you should think about what you're doing. No one likes to be bothered," he says calmly. He looks out at the valley. "The air is very clear in the morning. Hoang and I like to come up here to watch the sunrise." He smiles fondly at the boy.

The boy grins and reaches for his hand. Lester's pale bony fingers close around the boy's wrist.

"What are you doing here?"

"Resting. What are you doing here?"

"Fighting a war."

Lester smiles, then quickly rises to his feet. "As you can see, there's no war here."

Holding the boy's hand, he starts towards the trail. I watch the two of them start along the path, then follow them down to the clearing.

"What are we going to do?"

"We'll stick it out for another day then move on." I look at him appraisingly. "We could use the rest."

"You think it's okay here?"

"Seems to be."

"I wonder why?" he mutters, his glance fixes on the dark entrance way to the hut.

I pull off my right boot. The sock is wet and shredded. It tears away to reveal pale wrinkled flesh. I take a deep breath before I start on the other boot.

I'm trying to yank it off when the boy comes over and kneels in front of me. He grins, then pushes my hands away and tugs. I lean back and brace myself against the side of the hut.

The boy heaves backwards. The boot slides off with an agonizing slurp. Water trickles out of the boot.

My foot is unrecognizable. Its swollen and blistered. A dark crust of fungus is embedded between the toes. A watery stream of blood runs down my heel.

The boy crouches forward to look more closely. He raises his head and grins.

"Sit back." I glance up to see Lester standing behind me with a bucket of water.

"No, it's okay," I tell him, struggling to rise.

"Sit," he orders, and pushes me down. The boy moves out of the way as he kneels in front of me. He examines my foot, then gently runs his fingers over the swollen flesh.

He nods thoughtfully, then reaches into the bucket and removes a large green leaf. Dark liquid drips along the stem of the leaf.

"This will sting," he cautions, then wraps the leaf around my foot.

For a moment it feels warm and comforting. Then it begins to burn. I jerk my foot back "What the hell!"

"Sit still." He grabs my ankle and holds it in place as he wraps the rest of my foot in green leaves.

Loony wanders over to watch.

"What is that stuff?"

"Benzoin leaves. They'll draw out the poison."

"What the hell's a benzoin leaf?"

"It grows on a tree," Lester says, then rises and disappears into the hut.

Loony sits beside me. "How's it feel?"

"Better," I say in surprise.

"You see that picture he's got inside the hooch?" Loony shakes his head.

"You ever see anything like that?"

"Never."

"Maybe it all works for him," Loony says softly. "Maybe it's all a part of his scene."

"What scene?" I ask. "What the hell are you talking about?" But he rises without responding and walks into the hut. I hear the sound of Lester's voice, but can't make out the words.

The boy sits beside me as I clean my weapon. He watches intently as I break down and reassemble the 16. He sings that same tuneless song I first heard yesterday afternoon.

When I'm done, he rises and tugs on my hand. I hobble along behind as he leads me to the trail leading up to the peak. We start to climb. Ten yards into it he turns off the path and dives into the bush. His hand suddenly pops out of the leaves. His fingers open and close. I take his hand and he pulls me in.

I drop to my knees and follow as he moves easily through the twisted bramble.

We come into a small rocky clearing. The clearing is backed by a sheer incline leading all the way to the peak. The other three sides are enclosed by a vertiginous descent to the valley.

The boy moves to the center of the clearing and looks at me expectantly.

I limp over to his side. He nods, then points to the ground.

It's only then I notice the rocks.

Carefully placed in the ground, they map out a large circular design.

"What is this?"

The boy smiles and bobs his head from side to side.

I kneel and roll away one of the rocks. The earth beneath is loose and fertile. As I start to dig, the boy sits and begins to draw in the dirt.

After a few moments of digging, the smell hits me. It's a scent that no longer surprises me. I gag and lean back. The boy giggles. I bore down a few more inches until I'm sure, then I push the dirt back into the hole and replace the rock. I stand and hold out my hand. The boy drops his stick and reaches for me.

He's drawn two figures in the dirt. One tall, one normal in height. I can't tell if the two figures are fighting or embracing.

We walk out of the clearing and back to the hut.

"What'd you got up there, Lester?"

"Up where?" he asks innocently. We're in front of the hut. Loony is playing with the kid by the edge off the ridge. The boy's laughter carries over to us, punctuated by the deeper tones of Loony's appreciation.

"In that clearing up there, off the trail. The rocks. What is it?"

"He showed you!" Lester says in surprise, his gaze finds the boy.

"Yes."

"That's good. Only a month ago he refused to even go up there." He turns to me. His gaze offers nothing, only my own reflection.

"Who's up there?"

"How are your feet? Better?"

"Who do you have buried up there?"

"Innocence," Lester says softly.

I study him, trying to grasp the extent of his insanity.

How much of it is real? How much of it is simply convenient?

"Whose innocence?"

He smiles, then shrugs and says, "All of ours, of course."

He seemingly rises without moving. One moment he's beside me, the next he's striding across the clearing towards the valley trail.

"He's got bodies buried up there," I tell Loony, then wait for his explosion.

He shrugs and reaches for a cigarette.

"Hey, did you hear what I just said?"

"Yeah, so what?"

"So who the fuck's up there, and how come he's got them buried?"

"The kid's kind of cute."

"Loony, for Christ sake, listen to what I'm telling you here."

Smiling ruefully, he says, "You got to calm down, man. Just lay back and let it happen."

"Let what happen?" I ask, as he walks to the door of the hut.

"Hey, Hoang," he calls.

The kid runs out.

Loony swings him into the air. The kid's arms close around Loony's neck. Their laughter echoes around the clearing.

Lester doesn't reappear until late afternoon. He's carrying three fish, strung by their gills from a branch.

The boy runs to greet him. Lester smiles warmly and touches the kid's hair.

"Nice catch," Loony says admiringly

Lester nods in recognition of the compliment, then walks into the hut. Loony and the kid follow him inside.

We eat the fish for lunch. We sit in a circle outside the front of the hut. The boy hums as he eats. Loony keeps glancing at Lester. When he catches me watching, he blushes and looks away.

"We'll be moving out in the morning."

"No," Lester replies.

"What?"

"Your feet. You need at least another two days before you'll be able to move."

"That's not the way it's going to be," I tell him, holding his glance.

"What difference is another day or two going to make," Loony offers. We both ignore him.

"You should wait."

"Why?"

"Because you're not ready."

"I'm ready."

"No." He shakes his head sadly. "You only think you're ready."

"That's good enough for me."

Lester looks at the valley. When he turns back to me, he shakes his head and says, "We'll see."

"God dammit!" I explode, but Lester is already on the move, walking away from the fire.

"Take it easy," Loony tells me. "There's no need to be jumping all over the man's shit."

"What the hell's gotten into you?"

"Maybe something that ought to get into to you, too," he says cryptically, then turns and follows Lester.

The boy begins to sing. He's drawing in the dirt again.

When he's done, I don't bother to look. I simply wipe it away with my hand.

16

My mother and father are in the bedroom. He's yelling.

"How come he's so mad?"

John shrugs. He's eating a chicken leg. My mother's plate is empty. My father's plate still has two pieces of chicken and some potatoes.

"Maybe if he finished his dinner he wouldn't be so angry."

John makes a face.

I go back to my plate. My father is still shouting.

John starts to clear the table. I eat my last string bean and help. As we're putting the plates in the sink we hear the bedroom door open. I hear my father's footsteps in the hall. I run into the dining room to hide.

"What the hell are you doing!"

"Cleaning up," John mumbles.

"Well, god damnit, be careful!" my father snarls. I hear the front door slam and run into the kitchen.

John is at the window.

I moved to his side and see my father climb into his car. He pulls out and drives down the road.

"I'll bet you he's going to Klimas's."

John walks out of the room without answering.

I follow him down the hall to my parents bedroom.

"Mom," he calls.

My mother sniffles. "Yes, dear."

"Are you okay?"

"I'm fine. Why don't you and your brother finish eating."

"We already did."

"Then have some ice cream, and I'll be out in just a minute."

John leans forward and presses his ear to the door.

"Are you crying?"

"No, I'm not crying," my mother says, but I can tell she's lying.

John turns to me. "Go finish clearing the table."

"But what about the ice..." I stop when I see his face. I start towards the dining room. I glance back to see John opening the bedroom door.

"Mom?"

"Oh, baby," she cries, and John steps inside and closes the door behind him.

I sneak over and listen.

"It's all right, honey," my mother says. "It doesn't really hurt."

I hear someone start to cry.

I can't tell if it's my mother or my brother.

I run into the kitchen and fix a bowl of ice cream. I eat it in the dining room then carefully wash the bowl.

When I'm done, I clear the table, then go into the living room and wait for them to come out.

My mother is wearing her sunglasses.

"I finished clearing the table."

"Thank you very much," she says brightly.

John's face is red. He won't look at me.

We follow my mother into the kitchen and we wash and dry the dishes. I tell my mother she looks just like a movie star with her sun glasses on.

She puts down her dish cloth and looks at me. After a long moment, she smiles and touches the side of her face.

"You do," I insist. You're as pretty as Marilyn Malone."

"Monroe, stupid."

"I knew that."

"No, you didn't. You're too..."

"Boys," my mother cautions.

"I'm not stupid, am I?"

"No, dear, you're not stupid at all," my mother says, and touches my shoulder.

I grin at John.

He sneers and leaves the room. My mother watches him walk away.

"What's wrong with John?"

"He's just tired,' my mother says softly.

"Can I have some ice cream now?"

"Yes, you may."

I race to the refrigerator.

My mother goes into the other room. I hear her talking to John, but can't hear what she's saying.

After school the next day we walk out to John's fort.

John says, "Bad dog, you've been a very bad dog, and you have to be punished."

Prince whimpers.

"I'll give you a reason to cry!" he shouts, and then he hits her. His eyes look just like my father's.

When it's my turn I wonder if my eyes look that way, too.

Nancy has her own room. She has blue walls with flowers on them. We sit on the floor and lean against the side of her bed.

"Bobby's my best friend."

"He always calls me names, and he never lets me play with him," Nancy says.

"He's just being jerk."

"He says girls are stupid."

"Some girls are. Francine is," I say reasonably.

"But some boys are too." Nancy grins. "Bobby Shore is."

I crawl over to look at her bookshelf. There are dolls and books on all the shelves.

"That one is my favorite," Nancy says, and points to a blue book. "It's all about this girl who meets a prince, and he takes her far away to his kingdom."

There aren't any books about Indians or war. I move to her dresser and open a drawer.

"What are you doing?"

"Just looking."

"For what?"

"I don't know." The top drawer is filled with socks. There are all kinds of socks, all different colors.

I open the next drawer and reach inside. "I remember these." I hold up her blue shorts.

"It's getting too cold to wear shorts now."

I nod and go back to her drawers.

The next drawer is shirts. I close it and reach for the bottom drawer.

"Don't open that one."

I look over my shoulder and grin.

"Don't!"

Grinning at her, I slowly start to open the drawer.

"No!" she shouts, and throws herself at me. We staggers backwards and fall on the bed.

"Got you," I say, as I roll on top of her. Her legs wrap around my hips and she tries to kick me. I catch her hands and force them down.

She giggles and squirms beneath me.

"And what are you two doing?" Mrs. Helke asks. She's in the doorway, shaking her head and smiling.

Before I can answer, Nancy grunts and rolls to the side. She shouts triumphantly as I fall off the bed and hit the floor.

Mrs. Helke laughs. "C'mon, you two, I've got a surprise for you."

"What is it?" Nancy squeals.

I follow them downstairs.

"Now close your eyes."

We shut our eyes. Nancy's hand slips into mine as Mrs. Helke leads us into the dining room.

"Okay, you can open them!"

All the lights are off, and in the middle of the table is a huge chocolate chip cookie. In the center of the cookie are two white candles. The flames make shadows on the walls.

"Wow!" Nancy turns to me. Her eyes are huge.

"Is it your birthday?"

"No, silly."

"Is it your birthday, Mrs. Helke?"

"No, it's just..." Mrs. Helke pauses, then smiles. "...Tuesday."

We sit across from each other as Mrs. Helke cuts the cookie. She brings in two glasses of milk and sits with us as we eat. We tell her about school, and I tell her how I know almost all the state capitols, except for just a few.

When I look at Nancy, she has a chocolate chip stuck to the top of her lip. She keeps talking without even knowing it's there.

I peek over at Mrs. Helke and start laughing.

Nancy looks at me curiously, then looks at her mother.

Mrs. Helke starts to say something, then starts laughing, too. Nancy keeps looking at us, trying to figure out what's wrong.

We're laughing so hard we don't hear the front door open.

"What's all the laughing about?" Mr. Helke asks from the doorway.

"I don't know, they won't tell me," Nancy pouts.

Mr. Helke looks at her lip and smiles.

Nancy looks around the table. Her bottom lip starts to quiver.

I stop laughing. I'm afraid she's going to cry.

"It's okay," I whisper. "You have a chocolate chip stuck on your lip."

"That's not funny!" she wails, then leaps to her feet and runs out of the room.

"I'm sorry!" I yell, jumping from my chair. I start to follow her.

Mr. Helke catches me by the shoulder. "It's okay, she'll be all right."

"But she's crying."

"I'll talk to her." Mrs. Helke rises and leaves the room.

"It's okay to cry sometimes," Mr. Helke tells me. He's looking at me very closely. I want to tell him it's not okay to cry, crying is bad, but I can't find the words.

For a moment, I'm afraid I'm going to start crying.

"Why don't you sit down and finish your cookie." He leads me to my chair and stands behind me.

I sit very still. I'm afraid he's going to hit me.

I see his hand begin to rise out of the corner of my eye and duck to the side.

Mr. Helke looks at me for a moment, then very gently puts his hand on my back.

When Nancy and Mrs. Helke return, he's still there, his hand on my shoulder, not grabbing, just holding.

"Hi Daddy," Nancy says, and throws her arms around his waist.

Mr. Helke swings her in the air. "And how is my little Miss Chocolate Chip today."

Nancy giggles and throws her arms around his neck.

I sit at the table watching the three of them smiling at each other.

"Hi, Daddy," I say, and rush over to the door and throw my arms around my father's legs.

"What are you doing?" He shoves me away. "Did you break something?"

"I was just..."

"Don't lie to me, god dammit! If you broke something, I'm going to hear about it."

"I didn't break anything," I mumble, backing away.

He glares, then stalks out of the room. "Edna! What the hell is going on?"

I slip outside and run into the field. I don't stop until I get to the apple tree.

I lean against the trunk and stay there until my mother calls me for dinner.

My father doesn't say anything when I come inside, but I can feel his eyes watching me.

"What'd you do?" John asks, when I go into the bathroom to wash my hands.

"Nothing."

"Then how come you hugged him?"

"Use your napkin," my father growls.

John picks up his napkin and puts it in his lap.

"Can't you hold your fork the right way."

John shifts his fork, then looks at my father.

"Don't look at me like that. You know the right way to do it."

I check to see how I'm holding my fork.

"What happened at the office today?" my mother asks.

"Nothing happened at the office," my father snaps. "What makes you think something happened?"

"I don't know, I just thought..."

"You never think, Edna, that's the god damn problem around here. None of you ever... I thought I told you to hold that the correct way," my father says. His lips are tight. His eyes are locked on John.

John tries to adjust his fork. It falls and clatters to the table.

I keep my head down. I hear the sound of the slap.

"Jack," my mother sighs.

"What?"

"Let him eat," she pleads.

"He's not going to be allowed to eat if he can't eat correctly." My father turns to my brother.

"Now hold the god damn fork the right way or put it down."

John puts his fork down and looks at my father.

"All right, smart ass." My father raises his hand. The sound of the slap echoes around the room

"Jack!"

I peek over at my brother. His cheek is bright red.

"May I be excused?" John asks.

"Yes you..."

"No, you may not, god dammit. Not until I see you pick up that fork the right way."

John picks up his fork and holds it out for my father to see.

"Very good." My father nods. "Now eat the rest of your dinner."

"I'm not hungry."

"I didn't ask if you were hungry. I told you to eat."

John picks up his fork. We finish dinner silently.

"May I be excused now?"

"Don't you want any dessert?" my mother asks.

"If he wants to sulk, Edna, then just let him." My father turns on John. His eyes are bullets.

I look at my father. I look at John.

"What's for dessert?" I ask. My father turns on me.

"May I be excused?"

"Yes," my mother says quickly.

Before my father can say anything, John pushes back his chair and leaves the room.

"They''ve got to learn how to eat properly."

"I know they do, Jack," my mother says wearily.

"Well it's about god damn time they learned."

"May I be excused?"

"Don't you want dessert, either?"

"Just let them go. Let them both sulk upstairs," my father sneers.

I race out of the room.

"And stop running around the house, this isn't a gymnasium!" my father yells.

"Are you okay?"

"Yeah, just leave me alone."

I can hear my father's voice downstairs. He's still mad.

"You want to play cards?"

"No."

"You want to go outside and play?"

"It's too late. He wouldn't let us."

I walk over to the window. "Nancy has a room all to herself. She can see the lake from her window."

John turns on his back and looks at me.

"How come you didn't have any dessert?"

"I don't know."

"You always want dessert."

I shrug and look at my feet.

John shakes his head. His eyes are red. He looks like he's going to cry.

Before I can think of anything to say, he flips over on his stomach and buries his face in his pillow.

I sit on the edge of his bed. "It's okay, John. I didn't really want dessert anyway."

John's shoulder hitch.

17

I lean against the side of the hut and watch Loony wrestling with Hoang. Loony's stripped down to his t-shirt and shorts. His boots seem huge against the pale stem of his legs.

I have the letter to my brother on my lap. I just reread it, trying to recall what I wrote, and what I had wanted to write. All the words seem stilted and unreal. I can't remember what I was feeling when I wrote them. And after all that's happened, it's hard to imagine that other world even exists. It seems too far away to carry a presence into the world I now inhabit.

Loony's sitting on the kid's chest, tickling him.

"We need to check in."

Without bothering to reply, he rolls off the kid and goes into the hut. He comes out with the PRC and starts towards the trail.

"Hey, aren't you forgetting something?"

He looks over blankly.

I raise my weapon and wave it in the air.

He grins, shakes his head, then goes into the hut to retrieve his 16.

The kid disappears into the bush behind him.

I try to go back to my letter, but give up and put it away. I can't think of anything to write. I can't think of any way to explain this new insanity.

"Couldn't get through," Loony reports.
"How high did you go?"
"Little below the peak."
"See anything?"
"Nothing."
"What about Lester?"
"Not a thing." He shrugs. The kid tugs on the back of his t-shirt. Loony follows him over to the pig pen.

I watch the kid silently point to the pigs, then look up excitedly at Loony.

Loony crouches beside him. He throws an arm around the kid's shoulders. The two of them watch the pigs root in the mud.

Lester disappeared down the trail leading into the valley three hours ago. He left without saying anything.

I lean back and close my eyes and think about the rocks so carefully set in the circular design in the clearing above us. The pungent stench of decay rising from the earth.

What's buried up there?

"Innocence," Lester told me. "Our innocence."

What does it mean?

Does Lester even know, or he is so far gone he's completely abstracted himself from language?

"Loony?"

He swivels to face me.

"Did you see that clearing?"

"The one with the rocks?" The kid sits beside Loony and picks up his hand and plays with his fingers.

"Yeah, what'd you make of it?"

"What was I suppose to make of it?" He shrugs and pulls a cigarette.

"He's got bodies buried up there."

"So what. They're probably just grave markers."

"Marking whose graves?"

He smiles at the kid and traps his hand in his own. The kid giggles and rolls on his side. Loony runs a hand up the kid's legs to his chest and tickles him. The kid squeals delightedly.

"God dammit, are you listening to me?"

Startled, Loony turns. The kid's eyes watch us.

"Who the fuck's he got up there?"

"Only one way to find out," he says. He holds my eye, then rolls over on the kid. The two of them go back to wrestling.

I brace my back against the hut and push to my feet. I pick up the shotgun and start towards the trail. As I step into the bush, Hoang rushes over and grabs my arm. He braces his feet in the dirt and clings to me.

I try to pull away, but the kid hangs on, struggling to drag me back to the clearing.

Loony sits calmly against the hut watching us. The smoke from his cigarette rises in front of his eyes. He never blinks.

"Let go, would you?" I try to pull away.

The kid hangs on, violently shaking his head from side to side.

The anger comes out of nowhere. I feel it gathering, focusing on the kid.

The shotgun leaps into my hand and begins moving, starts to swing around...

"What do you think you are doing?"

Lester is at the foot of the valley trail, staring at me.

Before I can reply, the kid releases my hand and races to his side. He ducks behind Lester's leg and watches me.

"I was just going to take a walk." I deliberately keep the shotgun pointed at the ground.

"You shouldn't do that now."

"And why is that?"

"It'll be dark soon. And who knows what might be out there." He walks across the clearing and enters the hut.

After a moment, Loony rises and follows him inside.

We eat fish and rice, sitting in a circle outside the hut. The kid sits between Loony and Lester. Their bodies bracket the boy's, pressing against his sides.

I sit across from them, watching the three of them, desperately trying to understand what's happening.

Lester catches my eye. Smiling softly, he nods, then asks, "What's troubling you?"

"What are you doing here?" The question leaves my lips before I even know it's there. I feel the heavy press of the darkness behind me, as I wait for his response.

"What is it that I should be doing?" Lester shrugs expansively. His eyes never leave mine.

"What unit were you with?"

"Unit?" he says the word slowly, as if it no longer holds any meaning.

"What force then?" I say, unable to control my irritation. "Army, Marines, Air. What?"

Lester puts his arms around the kid's shoulder. He raises his gaze to mine then smiles and asks, "Where is your father?"

"What is this bullshit!" I throw my bowl to the ground. "What the fuck are you talking about?"

The kid's eyes seem to glitter across the darkness.

"Where is he?" Lester asks again. He watches patiently, waiting for my reply.

Shaking my head in disgust, I retreat from the fire.

"Where is your old man?" Loony asks curiously. "You never talk about him."

I ignore him and walk around to the back of the hut. Behind me, I hear Loony say, "Cleveland, he's got a little shoe store there. He does all right. When I get back, I'm going to..."

I shut out his voice. His words are meaningless here. There's no reality to anything he is saying. It's all wind and light.

I spread the groundsheet and lie down and look at the sky. A shadow moves above me and blocks the stars.

"How are your feet?"

"We're leaving in the morning."

"So you said." Lester crouches on his heels. The darkness hides his features, leaving only a darker expanse of space.

"You could come back with us."

"Back where?"

"Home."

"I am home," Lester says reasonably.

"You're real home. Not this..." I gesture disdainfully at the clearing, unable to find the proper words.

"This is my home. This is where my son and I will always live."

"Then this is where you'll die," I say brutally."

I wait a long time for his response.

"Your father is dead," is what Lester whispers.

"What the fuck are you talking about?"

"It's what all of our fathers have done." The darkness rises and towers over me. "They all died and left us alone to face their lies."

Before I can think of response, Lester glides into the darkness.

Loony wakes me.

"C'mon, man, we have to move," he says, prodding my shoulder.

I shake my head, trying to climb out of the dream.

"Where we going?"

He ignores me and quickly rolls up the groundsheet and shoves it under his arm. I stagger to my feet, still disoriented, angry with myself for having slept so soundly.

Loony waves me over to the hut.

"What's happening?"

"Just go inside." He pushes me through the door.

I stumble, regain my balance, see the groundsheet spread across the dirt floor, our packs against the wall.

"What the hell is..."

"Nothing," Loony says softly. "Just go back to sleep. It's okay now, man. Everything's all right. Don't worry."

"Worry about what?" I try to find his eyes in the darkness. Instead, I see Lester's shadow beside the doorway, watching us.

"It's okay?" Loony asks.

"Is what..." I stop when I realize he's not talking to me. He's talking to Lester.

Lester nods and disappears into the night.

"What the hell's going on, Loony?"

"Go to sleep. Everything's all right now."

I slump to the ground, struggling to keep awake, trying to understand what's happening.

Loony stretches out beside me. I hear his breath evening out. I listen to the silence around me, then lie down, thinking I'll rest for just a moment, then find out what the fuck is going on.

I close my eyes. The dream waits for me. It drags me down, displacing realities, until I can no longer tell which set of events is truly the nightmare.

18

On Saturday morning I wake before anyone else. I sneak downstairs and hold my breath as I walk by my parent's bedroom door

I eat a bowl of Cheerios, then wash and dry the bowl. When I'm done, it's only eight o'clock. It's still too early.

I tip toe into the living room. There is an empty brown bottle beside my father's chair. His ashtray is full of cigarette butts. I pick up one of the butts and pretend I'm smoking.

I hear a noise from upstairs and run into the kitchen to wait for John.

"Are you going over to Randy's?"

"You can't come."

"I don't want to."

"Why not?" he asks suspiciously.

I shrug and ask, "Are you going to leave a note?"

"Yeah."

"Could you leave a note for me, too?"

"Where you going?"

"Out," I say, then look at the clock. It's eight thirty. It must be time now.   "Out where?"

"Nancy's," I say, and open the screen door.

"Don't slam..." John whispers urgently.

But it's too late. The door slams shut.

"I'm sorry," I whisper.

John moves to the hallway and listens. After a moment he turns to glare at me.

"I got to go," I say, then race outside. I run through the field as fast as I can.

I sit in the front yard beneath an oak tree. I see Mrs. Helke walk past the kitchen window, then a moment later see Mr. Helke do the same.

I wonder if I should go over and knock. I start to rise, then sit back down. It might still be too early, and I don't want to make him mad. If he gets mad, he won't show me.

I lean back, trying to decide what to do.

I'm sprawled on the ground with a pile of leaves around me when I hear him come out.

"How long have you been out here?"

"Not long," I say, rolling over to look at him. I study his face closely, trying to see if he's mad. It's hard to tell, because I've only seen him mad that one time.

"Have you had breakfast?"

"I had a bowl of Cheerios."

"Why don't you come on inside while we eat."

I follow him to the front steps then stop. I kick the front of the porch and say, "Mr. Helke?"

"Yes." He crouches until he's right in front of my face.

I kick the stoop again. "Remember what you said the other day?"

He grins, then shakes his head and says, "About what?"

"About the car," I mutter, and risk a glance at his face.

He's smiling, but I'm not sure what kind of smile it is.

"You said that..." I pause, glance at him, then suddenly realize he's only pretending.

"I remember," he laughs. He puts his hand on my shoulder and pulls me into the house.

Nancy is at the kitchen table eating a bowl of Cheerios.

Mrs. Helke puts another bowl on the table.

I sit across from Nancy. She kicks my leg and grins. I grin back and pick up my spoon.

Nancy and I stand beside Mr. Helke's car. Mr. Helke opens the hood.

"Do you want to see?"

We both nod and move around to the front.

Mr. Helke grabs a wooden box and puts it by the fender. We climb up and look at the engine.

"Wow!" Nancy reaches to touch a wire. "Look at that!"

"Go ahead," Mr. Helke tells me. "You can touch it."

I touch the engine. My fingers come away greasy. I smear the grease between my fingers, marveling at how smooth it feels.

"When you're changing the oil, you have to be very careful not to spill. Do you remember why?"

"I do," I say quickly. "It's because oil never goes away. Right?"

Mr. Helke nods approvingly, then crouches to open his tool box.

Nancy and I jump down to watch. It's a long grey metal box, and inside are millions of gleaming tools.

"What this, daddy?"

"Those are vice grips."

"What do you do with them?"

"Here, I'll show you." Mr. Helke takes the vice grips and show us how they work. Nancy runs over to the side of the garage and fastens them to a piece of wood.

"Wow, look at that. You can't even get them off. Go ahead, try to take them off?"

No matter how hard I pull they won't come off.

"Watch this." She uses both hands to work the release. The grips open and come off easily. She looks over at me proudly.

We turn to see Mr. Helke slide beneath the car.

"Can we come under there too, daddy?"

"Just be careful."

We slide under the car.

"This is called the oil pan," Mr. Helke says, as he fits a wrench to a huge nut. He starts to turn the wrench.

"You want to try it, honey?"

Nancy giggles and reaches for the wrench.

"Not too much now," he cautions.

She turns the wrench. She looks at me excitedly.

"You want to try?"

I nod mutely.

Mr. Helke shuffles to the side so I can reach it. The steel handle is still warm from their hands. I start to turn the wrench. It wobbles and clatters on the cement floor.

"I'm sorry, I didn't mean to break it," I say quickly, ducking out of the way, trying to scramble from beneath the car.

Mr. Helke grabs my arm. "It's okay. Nothing's broken."

"I didn't mean it. Honest, I didn't."

"It's all right. It just fell, there's no harm done."

He picks up the wrench and fits it to the nut. "Here, try it again."

I slowly reach up to hold the wrench. It turns smoothly in my hands.

"Good job." Mr. Helke grins and pats my shoulder.

I blush and turn away.

After we're done changing the oil, Mrs. Helke makes peanut butter and jelly sandwiches. We eat outside beneath the oak tree.

"Fall's coming." Mr. Helke says. "Won't be long before the snow hits."

"I like snow," Nancy announces.

"Why's that, honey?"

"I like it when everything turns white."

Mrs. Helke touches her cheek.

"It's so pretty," Nancy says, then looks at me. "Don't you think it's pretty?"

"I guess." I shrug.

Mr. and Mrs. Helke laugh.

"I have to go home now and help John mow the lawn."

"Can I help?"

"Better not, my father might get mad." We're on the front steps. Mr. and Mrs. Helke are still by the oak tree.

"I'll see you later," I say, then walk over to the tree.

"Thank you for lunch."

"That's quite all right. You're welcome any time," Mrs. Helke tells me.

I nod, then kick a leaf and look at Mr. Helke. "Thank you for letting me change the oil, Mr. Helke." I kick another leaf, then add, "I'm sorry I drop the wrench."

Mr. Helke scrunches his eyes. "Did you drop something? I don't remember that. All I remember is what a big help you were."

I can't stop grinning.

"Good bye," I manage to blurt out, then run across their yard and down the road.

John's already mowing the front yard. When he sees me, he stops and waves me over.

"He's mad. Where were you all morning?"

"I was at Nancy's. Didn't you tell him?"

"I told him, but he's still mad."

"How mad?"

John shrugs and looks away.

I glance at the house. My father is standing at the kitchen window.

"You better go inside."

"Is he going to hit me?"

"He won't hit you. Just tell him the truth. Go ahead, it'll be okay."

I walk to the door then take a deep breath and open it.

"Where the hell have you been all day!"

"I was at Nancy's. I was helping Mr. Helke to..."

"You knew you were supposed to mow the lawn today."

My mother is in the hallway.

"Your brother's been out there doing your work for you. Do you think that's fair?"

"No, I don't think ..."

"That's right, you don't think," my father says. His lips are tight. His hand rises and crashes across my face.

I whimper and grab my cheek.

"Now get the hell out there and help your brother."

My father shoves me. I stumble outside.

"You want to push or rake?"

I'm still crying. "I don't care."

"He's watching."

I pick up the rake.

I move the cut grass into a pile. John pushes the lawn mower up and down the yard. My father stands in the window and watches us. He has a glass in his hand.

My mother brings out kool-aid. John turns off the lawn mower and we sit under the pear tree to drink it.

"Mr. Helke let me help him change his oil."

"He let you use his tools!" John says incredulously.

"Yep, he even let me take off the oil filter."

"What's that?"

"I don't know, but it's this white thing that goes in the engine."

"You got to go in the engine, too!"

"Yeah." I grin. "He let me do everything."

We both scramble to our feet when we hear the front door slam. My father comes around the corner of the house.

"You going to finish sometime today?"

"Yes, we were just.."

"I know what you were just doing. Now get the hell back to work," he says.

John starts the mower. I pick up the rake. My father watches, then goes around the side of the house. A few moments later we see his car drive down the road. We both watch as it turns into Klimas'.

"I hate Saturdays," John shouts as he pushes the lawn mower past me.

I remember changing the oil with Mr. Helke, the way he smiled, Nancy, and then my father's face.

"I hate them, too," I mutter.

Later we go to John's tree house.

John yells, "You never listen to me!"

I yell, "Where were you, god dammit!"

Prince squeals and races around the fort. He leaves bloody paw prints all over the floor.

19

I wake to the sound of voices, vaguely aware I've been hearing them for some time. The words suddenly take form. I leap forward, scrambling to my knees.

Loony's at the side of the entrance way. His terrified gaze finds mine.

Without taking my eyes off his, I reach to the side of the groundsheet. My hand glides across the dirt, encountering nothing.

I glance wildly around the floor of the hut. My weapon's gone.

I reach for my sidearm and find only an empty holster.

Loony nods to the entrance way.

I hold my hands out, palm up, asking the question.

He shakes his head. Small beads of perspiration glitter in the air.

I point to him.

He shakes his head again.

I hear Lester talking and crawl over to the door and peek out.

He's resting on his heels in the center of the clearing. Seated around him are VC regulars, a patrol group for the 2nd regiment.

I drop to my stomach in the dirt. I feel my heart pounding against my chest. I try to swallow the sudden wash of bile flooding my mouth.

Loony shifts his weight. I hear the soft creak of his boots. I hold my breath and stare outside, waiting for one of them to turn, to walk over and find us.

Loony catches my eye and opens and closes his fingers three times.

Thirty minutes.

I motion to the circle of men, looking at Loony quizzically.

He shrugs, then shakes his head.

I turn to the door when I hear the kid begin to sing. It's that same repetitive song. The sound is coming from the other side of the pig pen.

The kid skips into sight. He moves to Lester, touches his shoulder, giggles, then turns and looks into the hut.

I slither deeper into the shadows.

Lester's voice follows me. The awkward words flow fluently from his lips. I peer through the a crack in the wall and see the back of one of the VC. He's carrying American issue equipment. Canteen, 16, and dangling from his belt is an extra helmet. The words **THIS WAY OUT** are printed on the side of the helmet.

The kid's feet come into view. He's walking towards us.

I grab Loony's arm. My fingernails dig through his shirt and sink into his flesh. We stare at the doorway as the kids skips inside.

He's still singing. He grins and reaches for Loony.

"Hoang," Lester calls.

The kid throws us a disappointed glance, then backs out of the hut.

Sweat drips into my eyes. I smell the stale stench of my own breath.

One of the VC is speaking. His voice grows increasingly louder.

Lester responds, matching his tone.

They go on talking, their voices gaining strength, until they are both talking at the same time, trying to drown out the sound of the other.

One of the men rises and begins to walk around the clearing. His eyes are locked on the ground. I hear Loony's breath catch in his throat as the man suddenly crouches to examine the ground.

Hoang runs over and leaps on his back and laughs. The man grins and rises. He adjusts the weight of the kid, then begins galloping around the clearing. The other men's laughter follows them as the run from one end to the other.

Lester rests on his heels, smiling proudly as he watches Hoang and the man race around the clearing.

Lester abruptly turns and looks towards the hut. His gaze finds mine, his eyes bore into me. He nods, almost imperceptibly, then turns back to the circle.

I huddle against the side of the hut, watching him, watching them, waiting for it to happen, trying not to envision what they'll do to me.

Loony grunts softly.

I turn to see tears streaming down his cheeks. His eyes are screaming. He shakes his head, then curls up, clutching his knees to his chest. I hear the creak of his joints, see the hard white ridge of his knuckles, and listen to the voices coming from outside the door.

We lie on each side of the hut, trying to burrow into the lengthening shadows. The men outside are butchering one of the pigs. The kid is singing. Lester is rocking on his heels, smiling as he watches the carnage.

I'm welded in place. I can't move. I can barely breathe. I try to find some mental avenue into another world, any world. But it's all too distant, too detached from the smell of the men outside, the sound of their voices, and the kid's song, moving through my head like barbed wire.

One of the VC lights a cigarette. The smoke drifts through the doorway. A man moves away from his companions. He walks to the hut then turns and says something to Lester.

Lester nods agreeably and rises to his feet. He glides to the man's side and gestures towards the door.

I watch in horror as Lester calmly leads the man to the entrance way. He smiles, then motions to the door.

The man nods and steps forward.

I try to wrap myself in the shadows. My fingers dig into the earth, desperately clinging to it, willing it to hold my weight.

The VC steps inside. I feel his glance centering on my back. When he turns away, his eyes seem to leave a scorching wound that exits through my chest.

Lester touches the man's shoulder and whispers to him.

His voice screams across the silence.

Loony sobs.

Lester speaks again. He touches the man's arm, his shoulder. His hand gently closes around the man's neck, and he guides him around and out through the door.

I press my face into the dirt. I inhale the grit, feeling it become a part of my throat and lungs, until there's nothing left of me but the dark earth beneath me.

The kid sings outside. The men butcher the pig. Lester talks. His voice dances around the clearing.

By late evening the VC have packed up and started to move out. We watch from the hut as they disappear down the trail leading into the valley. Neither of us moves. Neither of us is able to move. Long after they've gone, we remained rooted in place.

"They were hungry," Lester announces. "They hadn't eaten in days." He squats in the center of the hut.

I manage to lift my head to look at him.

The kid skips through the doorway. He runs over to Loony and jumps on his back.

Loony shrieks and scrambles into a corner. His arms lock around his knees.

"It's okay." Lester glides to his side. "It's all right now," he says gently.

"What..." Loony shakes his head, grunts, stares incoherently at Lester.

Lester smiles and touches Loony's cheek. "You must be thirsty."

He takes Loony by the hand and the kid by the other, then leads them out of the hut.

I crawl to my knees and follow.

Loony sits with the kid on his lap. His arms are locked around the boy's chest. He has the point of his chin resting on the kid's head. He stares blankly into the sky.

"Where're the 16's?"

Lester is in front of me. His eyes keep trying to capture mine. I can't hold his glance, without feeling the rage building inside me.

"Why?"

"We could have been killed." The words seem awkward, too abstract.

"They could have killed us," I say more emphatically, struggling to find the proper phrasing.

"They didn't." He shrugs indifferently, then glances at Loony and the kid and smiles fondly.

"Fathers," he says, then shakes his head in admiration.

It moves through me so quickly I never have a chance to control it.

I lash out with my fist. The punch catches Lester on the lips. He falls back, raising a hand to his mouth. Blood drips through his fingers.

"What the fuck are you talking about! What the fuck do you think you're doing up here!"

I kick him in the side. "You could have fucking killed us, you cocksucking maniac." I throw myself at him.

My fingers are searching for purchase around his throat when Loony jerks me away.

Lester never moves, never fights. He just lies there, smiling at me, letting it all happen.

"Easy, man." Loony shoves me against the side of the hut. "Slow it down." His eyes are on my face, searching for a response.

Over Loony's shoulder, I see Lester lying in the dirt, still smiling with that same gentle beneficence.

I leap for him.

Loony slams me back in place. "Cool it, man. You're losing it."

"He fucking hung us out. He fucking burned us."

Loony's eyes lock on mine. He holds my gaze then shakes his head. There's a sadness to his gesture that finally shatters my rage. It's sudden depletion leaves me sagging in exhaustion. I slump to the ground.

Loony walks over to Lester and offers him his hand.

Lester slides to his feet. Still holding Loony's hand, he moves over and stops in front of me. He waits for my eyes, before he says, "In order to kill, one has to be able to see."

"What the fuck are you talking about?" I say wearily.

Before Lester can reply, Loony says, "They saw us, man."

I look up. Loony's eyes are feverish.

"You were there, man, you saw it. Fucking Charlie was looking right at us. No way he could have missed us."

I can still feel the burn of the VC's glance searing into my back and running through my chest.

"It's magic, man," Loony says softly. He looks in awe at Lester. "He's magic," he whispers.

Lester nods and walks across the clearing. The kid on one side, Loony on the other.

"But if all the fathers leave, what happens to the sons?" Loony asks. He sounds like an awe struck student seated at the feet of his master.

"Then the sons are lost," Lester replies sadly. "All that's left for them to believe are the lies they were told."

Lester is perched at the edge of the clearing, a hundred yards above the hut. Loony is beside him, his arm draped around the kid's shoulders. The sky is streaked with the bloody remains of the sun. The kid is humming softly.

I crouch in the brush, listening to them, trying to understand what's happening to Loony, to me, to all of us.

"Will they always be lost?"

"Yes."

"But that's not fair."

"No," Lester answers quietly. "It isn't."

"I don't understand what you're trying to say?" Loony shakes his head in confusion.

"Maybe you aren't suppose to," Lester says, then abruptly turns.

I crouch deeper into the bush. His gaze seems to pierce the bramble as well as me.

"Maybe there are some sons who have finally found the answers." Lester turns to Loony and pats his shoulder. "We have all been orphaned," he says, then rises and pulls Loony to his feet. "But it's the orphans now, who must decide how they want to live."

I watch them pass. Lester never takes his eyes from the path.

I lie on my back and watch the clouds shift across the sky, devouring what the sun has left behind, until all that remains is darkness.

20

"There's a good one," Bobby says. He picks up a hickory nut, peels off the green shell, and puts it in his bag. We've been collecting hickory nuts all afternoon. My mother uses them to make cakes for Christmas.

"Mr. Helke let me help him change the oil."

"My father lets me do that all the time. Doesn't your father let you help him?"

"My father never changes the oil. He always takes it to Mr. Cencula."

"My father says he can do it just as good, and it doesn't cost as much." Bobby picks a weed and chews on the end of it. "Maybe your father doesn't know how to fix cars."

"He knows how to fix them. He just doesn't want to get all dirty."

"My father doesn't get dirty," Bobby says quickly.

"You father was in the war."

"Yeah." Bobby nods. "He was a hero."

Mrs. Shore is outside raking leaves in the back yard.

"I got a full bag," Bobby holds up the hickory nuts.

"And I've got a yard full of leaves." Mrs. Shore leans against the rake.

"I'm sorry. I was going to do it, I just forgot."

"There's still time." Mrs. Shore smiles and hands him the rake then picks up the bag of hickory nuts. She looks inside. "You sure did get a lot of them, didn't you?"

Bobby smiles back at her.

We rake the leave into a huge pile then jump into it. When we climb out we see Bobby's little brother watching us. He's lying on the ground sucking his thumb.

"Hey Tommy."

Without removing his thumb, he smiles. A string of drool hangs from his chin.

"He still can't talk yet," Bobby says. Tommy throws his arms around Bobby's leg and hugs him.

Bobby giggles and falls on his back. Tommy hangs on, squealing excitedly.

Mr. Shore pulls into the drive. Tommy jumps up and runs over to the car. Mr. Shore grabs him and swings him in the air.

Mr. Shore walks over, carrying Tommy on his shoulders.

"I hope you boys are planning to clean that up."

"Yes, sir," Bobby says. "We were just playing is all."

He reaches over and ruffles Bobby's hair. "Play as long as like, but move it out by the road when you're done, all right?"

"Yes, sir."

We rake the leaves into a pile beside the street. Bobby runs into the house to get his father.

Mr. Shore comes out and tells us to stand back. He crouches before the pile, then pulls out a pack of matches.

We watch as the fire slowly begins to eat the leaves. A thick stream of smoke rises from the pile.

Mr. Shore moves over beside Bobby. His hand rises and rests on Bobby's shoulder.

We watch the fire until there's nothing left but gray ash.

For Sunday dinner we have roast chicken with mashed potatoes and broccoli. John and I like dark meat. My father likes white. My mother says she doesn't care. I get to have a whole leg.

My mother and father aren't talking. He doesn't seem mad, he just seems very tired. He keeps swaying in his chair. Once he even drops his fork on the floor. I pick it up for him, and he says thank you.

I say you're welcome and smile at John. He makes a face and rolls his eyes.

John and I help my mother clear the table. My father stays in his chair and finishes his drink.

My mother is telling us a story about when she was a little girl when my father comes out. He doesn't say anything. He just leans in the doorway and watches. We all get quiet.

"Go ahead with your story," he says, then suddenly reaches to grab the wall.   I start to laugh, then stop when I see his face.

"Well, my father, your grandfather was very mad."

"Did he hit you?"

"No, my father never hit us."

"What would he do?"

"He would send us to our room."

"That's not so bad," I say. "You could read your books or play with your toys, right?"

My mother grins, then looks at my father. He's still in the doorway. Only now he's using both hands to hold himself up.

"Are you okay, Jack?"

"Yeah, just tired." His hand slips and he stumbles into the kitchen. My mother rushes over and wraps her arm around his waist. My father straightens and pushes her away. "I'm all right."

"Why don't you go and sit down, and I'll bring you some coffee."

"Come in now," my father orders, and starts to turn. "And bring me another gin and tonic."

"Jack..."

"Edna," my father mimics, and disappears around the corner.

"Is daddy sick?"

"No, he's just tired." She pulls down a bottle and starts to make my father his drink. "You boys finish up in here. I'm going to go sit with your father for a while."

"What's wrong with daddy?" I ask, as soon as she leaves the room.

"He's drunk."

"Daddy's not drunk," I say, thinking of Otis on Andy Griffith. "He shaved."

John shakes his head, then turns to the sink.

"He isn't," I say again, but John never answers.

"My mother said it was all right."

"Really?" Nancy grins.

"Yeah."

She jumps off the swing and runs up the steps to her house. She's wearing blue jeans and a red shirt.

"Are you sure it's all right with your mother?" Mrs. Helke asks.

"She said it was okay."

"You watch your manners, young lady," Mrs. Helke warns.

Nancy bobs her head, then races across the yard. I catch up with her on the road. We take the path through the field. Nancy stops beneath the apple tree and points. "That's where I fell."

"That was a long time ago."

"I still have a scar. You want to see?"

"No, you already showed it to me."

She keeps staring at the branch.

"You want to go up?"

She shakes her head.

I climb up to the first branch and reach for her hand.

"I don't want to." She backs away.

"If you promise not tell anybody, I'll tell you a secret?"

"What?"

"First you have to promise."

"I promise." She takes a steps closer to the tree.

"I got stuck up here."

"No, you didn't. You're just saying that to make me feel better."

"I did. John had to help me down. He saved my life."

"You saved my life, too."

"Come on up," I say again, and reach for her.

Nancy shakes her head, but doesn't move away.

"I promise I'll hold on to you."

"Promise?"

"Cross my heart."

Nancy reaches for my hand. "You won't let go?" she asks. She's biting her lip.

"I won't let go."

She puts her foot against the trunk of the tree. I pull. She rises, then wraps herself around the branch. She takes a deep breath and reaches out to grab my arm. Her fingers dig into my muscle as she slowly straightens.

"It's not that high," she says, starting to smile. She laughs, then suddenly stands and walks along the branch.

I keep watching her. I'm afraid she's going to fall again.

She swings to the ground and looks up at me.

"What're you waiting for?" she says, then turns and runs up the path to my house.

It's Monday night. My father is bowling. We're having hamburgers and french fries. Nancy gets to sit in my father's chair. John keeps looking at her, then looking at me.

"What's wrong?" I finally ask.

John grins.

"Make him stop, mom."

"You're brother isn't doing anything. Just leave him alone. Nancy, would you like some more french fries?"

"No, thank you."

"Are you sure? You hardly ate anything at all."

"I'm not very hungry," Nancy says, then suddenly giggles and looks at me.   I start laughing too.

My mother shakes her head and passes the french fries to John.

Because Nancy's there, we get to have ice cream and brownies for desert.

When we're done, my mother says, "Since your brother has a guest tonight, why don't you and I do the dishes."

"That's not fair."

"When you have a guest, you won't have to do the dishes either."

"Then I want Randy to come over next Monday night."

"Why don't you have him come over sometime this week?" my mother asks.

John shrugs and looks at the floor.

"Fine, you can have Randy next Monday."

John grins and starts clearing the table.

"Just there and back," my mother warns. "And stay to the side of the road."

I promise her I will, then open the door.

"Thank you for having me for dinner."

"You're very welcome, Nancy."

"Bye." Nancy waves at John.

John blushes, then nods and turns back to the sink. I hear my mother's laughter as I close the door.

We run across the yard and take the short cut through the field. The sun is just starting to set.

"I like your mother," Nancy says. "She's nice."

"I like her, too," I answer, looking at the shadows along the path. They're creepy looking. I think about walking home alone, and decide I'd better take the road the way my mother told me to.

When we pass the apple tree, Nancy reaches for my hand. I don't say anything, but I hold her hand just as tightly as she's holding mine.

When we get to her house, she wants to kiss me again.

"How come?"

"I don't know." She shrugs.

"Well, maybe a little one.

"On the lips?"

"All right, on the lips."

She taste like hamburgers.

When we step back, she grins and says, "Now we have to get married."

"Okay," I say. "See you tomorrow."

"Do you like her?"

"She's okay, for a girl."

"You want to hear a secret?"

"What?"

"You have to promise you won't tell mom and dad."

"I won't tell."

"We're going to get married," I whisper. "She asked me tonight."

"What'd you say?"

"I said I would."

John shuffles back on his pillow without saying anything. He opens his book.

I pull the blanket up to my chin and watch him read.

"John?"

"Yeah?"

"You can come live with us when we get married," I say, then roll over on my side and close my eyes.

21

Loony has cut a three foot section of bamboo into a semblance of a baseball bat. The kid holds it, resting its length on his shoulder. For a ball, he's knotted four pairs of socks. He pitches the socks to the kid and yells, "Swing."

The kid giggles and never lifts the bamboo bat from his shoulder.

Loony shakes his head patiently, then picks up the sock and tries again, with the same results.

I stretch my legs out in front of me and shift my feet into the sun. The right one is completely healed. The left one is almost back to normal. The swelling is gone. When I flex my toes, the flesh moves without cracking or bleeding.

I lie back and close my eyes. The sun lights up the darkness behind my eyelids. The heat presses down on me with a reassuring weight. I give in to the pressure, luxuriating in the warmth.

Lester is inside the hut. I can hear him whistling. It's the same tuneless song the kid is always singing.

"I'll put these up there," Lester says, as he appears in the doorway. He's carrying our sidearms and M-16's. He points to the roof of the hut. "I don't want Hoang playing with them," he adds, then carefully balances our weapons on the thatched roof.

He crouches beside me and sits on his heels. We watch Loony and the kid.

"He's very good with the boy, isn't he?"

I nod, unable to find the energy to speak.

He leans over to examine my feet. "They look good. Another couple of days and you'll be able to get around without any problem."

I watch the kid swing the bamboo bat. He hits the socks. The socks roll a foot in front of him and stop.

Loony yells excitedly.

The kid runs over and wraps his arms around Loony's leg. Loony swings him into the air. The kid's laughter sings all around us.

I think about rising to get some water. I glance at my legs, think about drawing them back, planting them, then pushing to my feet.

Too much effort, I decide, and shift more comfortably against the wall.

Lester flows to his feet. He moves around the back of the hut.

When he reappears, he's carrying a bucket of water. He places it beside me and fills the ladle.

"Drink," he says. "You must be thirsty."

Without questioning his prescience, I bow over the wooden ladle and sip the cool liquid.

"We should've called it in," Loony says, after Lester and the kid make their way up the trail towards the peak.

I shrug, too comfortable to speak.

"Don't you think we should've called it in?"

"I don't know," I reply, without even thinking about his question. It's one that commands too much thought, and it all seems too complicated to unravel.

"But they were 2nd regiment," Loony says. "And they were moving north."

"So?"

"So, I thought that's what we were doing out here."

"What?" I ask, genuinely curious.

"Watching for movement," he says patiently, then a moment later adds, "Are you okay?"

"Yeah, I'm fine." I lean back and close my eyes. I hear Loony asking another question, but the heat of the sun burns its way into me. It presses against me with an almost sensual weight. I open myself to its arms and sleep.

When I wake, the sun is just touching the western peaks. It's grown cool. I stagger to my feet and enter the hut. I unroll the groundsheet and wrap it around my shoulders.

Coming back outside, I suddenly become aware of the silence. It's so absolute that even the sound of my breathing seems to violate its presence.

I pause, holding my breath, finding an obscure solace in this vacuum where even I am not able to exist.

The scream of a monkey shatters the illusion. A bird shrieks as it soars over the ridge. I hear the flap of its wings as it struggles against the currents.

Clutching the groundsheet around my shoulders, I start up the path.

The three of them are sitting on the ledge, watching the sunset. The boy is between them. Each of them has an arm around the kid's shoulders.

Loony turns and grins. He shuffles to the side and I sit beside him.

"It's really fucking beautiful, man," Loony says, turning back to the wash of colors drowning the sky.

I look out and silently agree.

"And Alexander wept when he looked upon all the lands he ruled, and realized there were no more worlds to conqueror," Lester says quietly.

I look across the fire and catch his eye.

"There are always going to be wars, and always soldiers bred to fight them." He smiles sadly. "But it's the fathers who stay home, weeping their crocodile tears for all the sons that will never return."

"Right on," Loony whispers in agreement. His gaze is locked on Lester's face.

"Wars aren't fought over geography or ideology. They're born in the hearts of the fathers when they look at their sons and see the strength of their innocence. It's that innocence they wish to conquer. They need to destroy it. Because if it exists in their sons, then it must have once existed in them. And if it can't be recovered, then it can't be allowed to survive."

Lester's eyes hold me.

I break away from his glance and hold out my hand to Loony. He pulls a cigarette. I use a stick to light it, then watch the flame devour the twig.

"You're a soldier."

Lester shakes his head.

I point to his tags.

He glances down at his chest and seems surprised by the sight of his dog tags. He examines them for a moment, then with a sudden wrench of his hand rips them away and throws them into the fire.

I watch the metal begin to curl and blacken.

"What do you want?" I whisper.

Lester shrugs and rises to his feet until he towers over us.

"What?" I ask again.

Without responding, he turns and disappears into the hut.

"He's magic," Loony whispers. "Fucking magic."

I sit alone by the dying embers of the fire. Loony is inside the hut with Hoang and Lester. I have the letter to my brother on my lap. I can't make out the words. All I can see is a scrawled line of ink trailing across the page. I remember when it was made, but can't remember making it.

I place the point of my pen against the paper and wait for the words to come.

I write: `I am here now.' then carefully replace the letter in my pocket.

Time drifts with the shading of the day. Light, dark, dusk.

I rise, shuffle out of the hut, eat, bask in the sun, eat again, then yet again, and sleep.

The world slows into an acute magnification of Loony, the kid, and Lester. I listen to the sound of their voices, but feel no compunction to respond to their words.

After a while, they leave me alone. I watch them. I watch the way their bodies function. The movement of their arms and legs. The elasticity of their flesh.

The kid is sitting on my lap. He's singing, rocking back and forth. Loony peers down at me worriedly. He says something, I nod. He goes away. The kid resumes his song.

Lester is beside me. His hand is holding mine. His hand is so much longer than mine, so much paler. I can almost follow the thread of his veins as they wind along his wrist and up his arm. His voice is gentle. I close my eyes and let its rhythm lull me.

It's Lester who finally breaks through my lethargy.

"I have to go," he says.

His words shatter my silence. I feel the torpid slither of fear gathering along the pit of my stomach.

"Why?" I ask, then shake my head, and ask, "Where?"

"Away." He smiles softly. "It is time."

"Time for what?" My voice is hoarse from lack of use.

"Just time." He shrugs. He's carrying a VC pack strapped to his back.

"I want you and Loony to watch Hoang while I'm gone."

I rise awkwardly to my feet. My legs tremble with the effort.

"You're coming back, aren't you?"

"Of course." He touches my shoulder. "Where else would I go?"

"How long will you be gone?"

"Days. No more than days."

"What will we..." I pause, suddenly finding the question I'm about to ask too strange to utter.

"Do?" Lester says gently, then shakes his head patiently. "You will do whatever is necessary."

"What's necessary?" I ask, but he turns without answering.

I watch him start down the trail towards the valley. By the time I reach the ledge, he's disappeared from sight.

"Well, where the fuck was he going?"

"I don't know."

"You didn't ask?" Loony says incredulously.

"No, I don't think I did."

"Why the fuck not?"

Before I can reply, Loony's starts to pace. "What the fuck are we supposed to do now?"

"He wants us to watch the kid." I look over at Hoang. He's in the doorway of the hut, silhouetted by the sun.

"For how long?"

"A few days."

"Then what?" Loony stops in front of me. His eyes crawl up my face and settle on mine.

"Then we do something else." I shrug and turn away.

"What?"

"I don't know, what ever the hell we're supposed to do," I reply, surprised by my sudden anger, and even more surprised by how welcomed it feels.

When I turn back to Loony, he's looking at me quizzically.

"What?"

Loony breaks away from my glance and shakes his head. "Nothing," he says, and walks over to the kid. He crouches in front of him and holds out his arms.

The kid moves into the circle of Loony's arms, and Loony's arms close, trapping the boy in his embrace.

Loony and the kid start up the trail. They both look back at me, surprised by my refusal to accompany them.

As soon as they're out of sight, I pull down the weapons from the roof.

I sit with the 16's on my lap and begin to clean and oil them. My hands move with a familiarity I find reassuring. I do the same with the shotguns and .45's.

When they return, I'm sitting outside the hut. I have all our weapons laid out on the groundsheet. They gleam brightly in the failing light of the sun.

Loony stops beside me.

When I look up, he asks, "Is it time?"

"Yeah," I say, "It's way past fucking time."

He nods, then drops to his knees. The kid curls up in his lap. Loony reaches out tentatively. His fingers lightly trace the outline of a shotgun then close around the barrel. He hefts it appraisingly, then swings it to his shoulder.

The kid begins to sing.

I pick up a 16 and am surprised by the sudden tight, almost painful stretch of my lips.

I look at Loony. He's ginning fiercely. His hands are locked around the shotgun.

He starts to laugh.

The kid sings.

The stock of the rifle rises and nestles beneath my arm. It fits snugly against my side, blending in with the gathering night.

22

Mrs. Sherwood leaves me alone. She doesn't ask me any questions all morning. She doesn't even look at me.

At recess, I meet John in the bathroom and tell him.

"Do you still hate her?"

"Yes."

"That's why she's not bothering you."

"I hate her a lot," I tell him as he walks out the door.

David Magnus is talking to Bobby. They're standing at the edge of the playground.

"What are you doing?"

Bobby shrugs and looks away.

"Who wants to know?" David sneers.

We're the same age, but he's in Mr. Neubauer's class.

"How come you're so little?" David turns on me.

"I'm as big as you are."

"No, you're not. You're just a runt."

"Take that back."

"Make me." David moves closer. His hands are curled into fists.

I look at Bobby. Bobby shrugs and kicks an acorn.

"Chicken," David says, and shoves me.

Before I now what I'm doing, I bend over and run at him.

"Fight! Fight!" I hear someone yell, as I crash into David. We hit the side of the building, then fall to the ground. I'm on top, wrestling with him, when he punches me in the side of the head.

"That's not fair!" I yell.

"Hit him back!" Bobby shouts.

I make a fist and hit David in the side. His bones hurt my knuckles.

He makes a noise and rolls away from me. He gets to his feet at the same time I do. There's a circle of kids around us. I see John, and then I see Nancy.

David tries to hit me. I skip out of the way.

"Get him!" John yells.

"Punch him!" Nancy screams.

I hit him on the arm. David lashes out and hits me in the nose. For a moment my nose is numb. I reach up to touch it, then stare at my fingers. They're all bloody.

"Had enough?" David asks.

I leap at him, windmilling my arms. He staggers backwards. I hear Nancy yell, then suddenly see her jump on David's back. I'm so surprised to see her, I stop fighting.

She slaps his head and shoulders. David crouches over and screams, "Get her off of me."

"Here comes a teacher," John yells.

I grab Nancy by the waist and pull her away, just as Mr. Shafer comes around the corner.

"What's going on?"

Nobody answers.

"Who's fighting?" he asks.

We all look at our feet.

He reaches over and lifts my chin. "Your nose is bleeding," he says, and waits for me to say something.

After a moment, he shakes his head and pushes me towards the school. "Go see the nurse."

I start across the playground.

I hear Mr. Shafer telling everyone there is no fighting allowed. The bell rings and everyone runs towards the doors.

When I look back, Mr. Shafer is the only one left on the playground.

The nurse makes me lie on my back and hold a wet cloth to my nose. She's wearing a white dress and a white hat. Even her shoes are white. She gets some of my blood on the front of her dress. I tell her she should wear a red dress tomorrow, that way when she gets bloody it won't show. She tells me to be quiet and to lie back down.

I like being in the nurse's office. It's very quiet. I get to lie down, and I don't have to hate anybody.

Mrs. Sherwood is outside the classroom when I come back. I give her the note from the nurse.

She makes a noise in her throat, and tells me I'm troublemaker, and I'll always be a troublemaker.

I don't say anything. I just nod and wait for her to finish.

"Go sit down, and I don't want to hear another word out of you for the rest of the day."

I open the top of my desk to get my Reading book. I can feel Mrs. Sherwood watching me, but I never look up. I don't look at her for the rest of the day. I know her eyes are waiting for me.

"How come you did that?"

"He made me mad."

"Why? He didn't hit you. He hit me."

"But he made you bleed," she says.

When I look over, it looks like she's going to cry.

I pick up a rock and throw it into the field. Nancy's hand crawls across the dirt and touches mine.

"Did it hurt a lot?"

I shrug.

"You were very brave."

"Lets go down to the lake."

We run along the path to the lake. The wind is blowing across the water. The waves are very large. Nancy wraps her arms around her chest. She's wearing a white shirt and jeans.

"It's cold."

"Winter's coming."

"And snow." She grins.

"Yeah," I say. "Snow, too."

"Then we can go sledding at Klimas's."

"We have to wait for the ice to freeze," I remind her.

"I know that." She puts her hands on her hips and glares at me. She looks just like Mrs. Helke when she does that.

I wonder if I looked like my father when I hit David.

We go back to her house and up to her room. Nancy lies on her bed and looks at the ceiling. I lie on my back on the floor.

"What are you two doing?" Mrs. Helke is in the doorway.

"We're pretending we're dead."

"I got shot in the war," I tell her.

"I fell out of an airplane in Pittsburgh," Nancy explains.

Mrs. Helke shakes her head and says, "Well, I guess if you're both dead, I might as well put those cookies away."

"Cookies!" Nancy yells, and leaps off the bed.

I follow her downstairs into the kitchen.

"You know," Mr. Helke says. "If you ever want to talk about anything. I'd be willing to listen."

"Talk about what?" I ask. We're at the edge of his yard. I can see Mrs. Helke in the kitchen window watching us.

"Oh, I don't know," Mr. Helke says. "Anything that might be bothering you."

"Nothing's bothering me."

"Well, if something ever does." He touches my shoulder. "I want you to know you can always talk to me about it."

"Thank you."

"You're welcome." He smiles.

"I've got to go now."

"Okay, be careful going home."

I start down the road. When I hear the Helke's door close, I race back to their house. I crouch and move around the side until I'm below their dining room window. It's getting dark, and I know I have to hurry or else I'll get in trouble.

I peek through a corner of the window. Mr. and Mrs. Helke are at each end of the table. Nancy is sitting in the middle with her back to me. Mr. Helke is talking, but I can't hear the words.

Nancy looks at her father and says something. Mrs. Helke laughs and reaches over to touch her. Nancy giggles and keeps talking. They're all smiling, talking, and eating.

I creep away from the side of their house and run home.

My father is in the kitchen. He's at the table watching my mother cook.

"Go wash up, we're going to eat soon," my mother says.

My father nods to me. He's resting his drink on his knee.

I wash my hands and start towards kitchen.

"No," my father says. "I want some time alone with your mother." He points to the other room.

I go into the living room and sit on the couch. I look at a magazine until it's time for dinner.

"Couple of advisor were killed," my father says to my mother. "This'll just be the beginning. You wait and see."

"I don't think we're going to get involved. We're not that..."

"God dammit, put you napkin in your lap," my father yells.

"I'm sorry," I mutter, and spread my napkin across my knees. I keep my eyes on the table. I can feel my father's eyes burning into me.

John nudges my foot.

"What were you saying?" My father turns back to my mother.

I relax and reach for my milk. My finger hits my plate and trips. Before I can help it, my hand bumps into my glass.

"I'm sorry!" I yell, watching the milk spill across the table.

My father hits me.

I start to cry.

"Stop that right now, or I'll give you something to cry about."

"I didn't mean it," I say, then sob.

My father hits me again.

I can't stop crying.

"Jack..."

"You stay out of this. They're spoiled enough as it is," my father tells her. His lips are tight. He raises his hand. I cringe.

"Go up to your room, right now."

"But I..."

He glares at me, daring me to say something.

I stumble away from the able and run up the stairs.

"Knock knock?" John says. My parents are downstairs watching TV. John has his flashlight on.

When I don't answer, he shines it at me.

"Knock knock?" he says again.

"Who's there?"

"Boo."

"Boo who?"

"How come you're crying." He grins

I sniffle, and say, "I'm hungry."

"He'll get mad."

"But I'm hungry."

"Knock knock?" John says.

"I want something to eat."

"Wait'll they go to bed, and I'll sneak down and get you something."

"You promise?"

"Yeah, I promise. Now, Knock knock?"

"Who's there?"

"Who."

"Who who?"

"What are you an owl?" John says, and waits for me to smile.

He tells me three more knock knock jokes, and then goes back to his book.

I close my eyes and try to sleep, but my stomach won't let me. It keeps making noises.

I creep over to the side of his bed and shake his shoulder. When he opens his eyes, I say, "You promised."

"Go back to sleep."

"But you promised."

He looks at me for a moment, then sits up and rubs his eyes.

"I'm really hungry, John."

"All right, don't cry."

"I'm not going to cry," I sniffle. "But I'm so hungry." I rub my stomach.

He walks over to the doorway, peeks down the stairs, then slips around the corner.

When he comes back, he's out of breath and grinning. He has his shirt rolled up in front.

"Look what I got," he says, and lets go of his pajama top. Three carrots, four chocolate chip cookies, and a banana fall out on the bed.

I grab a cookie and shove the whole thing in my mouth.

We sit in the middle of our room and spread the food out on my pillow. John stands his flashlight up on its end, so that it shines on the ceiling. We eat and make hand shadows.

We're both laughing when we hear my parents door open. We hold our breaths and listen.

Footsteps start down the hall. As soon as the bathroom door closes, we scramble into our beds.

I close my eyes, praying he won't come up.

My parents door opens and closes.

"Did you eat enough?"

"Yeah."

"Go to sleep now."

"Thank you," I say, and curl up beneath my blankets. It feels warm and safe there. My stomach is quiet. I can hear my brother breathing across the room. I close my eyes. I hear the click of John's flashlight, the pages of his book turning.

23

I stop in the center of the clearing and examine the rocks. There are thirteen of them forming a circle, another two are set inside.

I hear Loony moving through the bush behind me.

"What do you think?" he asks. The kid is beside him, one arm looped around Loony's waist. "You want to dig it up?"

"No," I say uncertainly. "I don't think I do,"

"Then lets go up." Loony motions to the peak. The kid smiles and reaches to touch the barrel of my shotgun. I swing it to my shoulder and walk out to the path.

Loony picks up the PRC and we trudge up to the ledge, overlooking the valley.

"What do you want me to tell them?"

"Tell them we're coming in," I reply, looking out at the valley, wondering about Lester.

He's been gone four days now, and we're ready to do what we have to do.

I hear Loony raising base. The kid kneels beside the radio. He grins as he runs his fingers along its sides.

"Black Fox returning," Loony says, then disconnects.

We clean and oil our weapons, stock our packs, and wait for Lester. The kid sings. Loony paces impatiently around the clearing. He pauses at the ledge, searches the valley below, then begins pacing again.

I watch him from the side of the hooch and wait for Lester to return.

I take the path down into the valley. I move silently through the bush with an agility I've never known before. The land becomes a part of me. Its contours impress themselves upon my brain and body.

I glide effortlessly through the razor edge stalks of the elephant grass. My feet move gracefully along the rocky ground. The blue bowl of the sky fits comfortably above me, as the country below slowly unveils its secrets.

There is no longer any fear, there is only the sense of my return, of my becoming a part of what I have always been.

"Nothing," I say, as I come into the clearing.

Loony shakes his head in disgust. The kid looks up curiously.

Loony disappears into the hut.

The kid looks at me, then begins to sing.

I lean against the side of the hut and listen to his song.

"How much longer?" Loony asks.

We're seated in front of the hut. Loony on one side of the fire, me across from him, the kid to the side.

"Got to be soon."

"Place is starting to get to me," he says, glancing around nervously. He pulls his cigarettes. We light up. The kid eyes follow our hands.

"Maybe we should..." I stop as the kid leaps to his feet and races to the edge of the clearing.

I roll away from the fire and flatten on my stomach, the shotgun trained on the path. I see Loony off to my right, his 16 leveled in front of him.

I hear the song, look at the kid, and see him turning to look at me bewilderedly.

Lester comes into view. His pale features take form as he steps out from the shadows. The kid runs to him and throws his arms around his legs. Lester grins down at him.

A little girl steps out from behind him. She's singing. Her eyes trail across the clearing, pause on me, then Loony, then turn back to Lester.

Lester takes her by the shoulder and leads her to the fire. Hoang follows, staring intently at the little girl's back.

"You are prepared," Lester says, his gaze taking in our weapons.

"We're ready," I tell him, rising to my feet.

"I'm glad." He nods to both of us, then moves into the hut. The children follow him inside.

I catch Loony's glance and shake my head.

"What the fuck's that all about?" he mutters, then disappears through the doorway.

When I hear Lester begin to talk, I move to the other side of the clearing. I don't want to hear him. I don't want to know what he's saying.

I smoke, look at the stars, and watch the darkness flow up the side of the mountain.

"We're leaving," I tell him in the morning.

"When?"

"Tomorrow."

Lester nods thoughtfully. "That gives us enough time."

"Time for what?"

"For what we all have to do?" He smiles.

Loony is leaning in the doorway of the hut. The little girl is seated between his legs, Hoang is perched on his knee.

"And what the hell's that?"

"It's all empty," Lester says, turning and gesturing to the land around us. "But it's all we have left now. Everything else is gone. And what we have left, is not enough. It's never enough," he concludes sadly. He steps over to the side of the hut.

"Come back with us," I say, following him, planting myself in front of him.

"We are all orphans. One by one, all of our fathers have gone away and sent us to this savage place. And now that they're gone, there's nowhere else for us to go. It's up to us to protect what we have." His eyes hold me. "Don't you understand?" he whispers feverishly.

"We're leaving in the morning. Do whatever the hell you want."

"I'm going out," I tell Loony, then turn and slide into the bush.

I hear the kids begin to sing. And before I'm out of range, I hear Loony's voice rising to join theirs.

I moved down the path into the valley. I stumble over a rock and fall to my knees. I rise and move on.

The elephant grass towers above me. I step into it. The stalks slash at me, slicing into my hands and face.

I stagger into a clearing, a cloud of mosquitoes swarms my head. I feel them delicately puncturing my flesh, sucking my blood.

I lurch forward, stumbling across the valley floor. Sweat beads along my forehead and drips into my eyes. It blinds me, blurring my vision, until all I can see or feel is the sudden resurgence of fear. It crashes into me and leaves me cowering behind a rock, clutching my weapon to my chest, trying to digest my terror.

I rise and run blindly into the bush. I trip over a log, see the earth rising towards me. I shriek as it thuds into my chest. I cover my head, cowering, waiting for the explosion, waiting for the hot bits of metal to rip me apart.

"The fathers," I whisper, staring frantically through the bamboo shoots, hearing the sound of movement. The thud of their footsteps. The alcoholic stink of their breath as they exhale death.

I curl on my side, turning my body into itself, until I slowly disappear into the dark cavern of my own flesh.

And it is there, in the darkness of my own arms, that they finally appear to me. All of them, parading before me.

The fathers.

The ones who died, the ones who disappeared, and all the ones who lied to us and led us here.

All of them conspiring with their silence and rage to bring us to this barbarity.

The fathers.

Our fathers.

My father...

24

I sit at my desk and read my Geography book. I read about Australia, and try to hate Mrs. Sherwood at the same time.

She leaves me alone, so I guess I'm hating her hard enough.

I go down by the summer house and sit on the pier. I watch my father row across the lake. He has a cigarette in his mouth. He stops to drink from his beer, then picks up his fishing pole and starts to fish. I lie on my stomach and watch.

When it starts to get dark, I run across Mr. Welty's yard to wait for him. I hear the creak of his oars growing closer. I wonder how many fish he caught.

The creaking sound suddenly changes. I listen carefully, then run across Mr. Welty's yard to Klimas's.

My father's boat is pulled up on the sand. I race up the stairs and peek through the window. My father at the bar with a drink in front of him. He picks up his glass and glances towards the window. I duck and run down the hill.

When my mother asks, I say, "Daddy's fishing."

She turns back to the stove.

John gets to sleep over at Randy's house. I'm all alone with my mother and father. We eat dinner, and then I help my mother with the dishes. We sit in the living room and watch Gunsmoke.

I sit beside her on the couch. I lean against her side and she puts her arm around my shoulders. Her hand rests on my elbow. I reach over and play with her fingers.

"Don't do that."

My father turns to look at me. I sit very still and stare at the TV until I feel him turn away.

I lie on John's bed and look at the ceiling. His pillow smells different then mine. I find his book, then grab his flashlight and carry it back to my bed. I like my bed better.

I read his book until I fall asleep.

When I wake up the flashlight is still on. Only not as bright. I turn it off and sneak it back under his mattress.

Bobby tells me his mother and father are going to Florida.

"Tallahassee," I say.

"What's that?"

"The capital of Florida."

"Who cares." Bobby makes a face. "They're going to be gone two whole weeks."

"Who's going to watch you?"

"My aunt Debbie," he says, then reaches into his pocket and holds up a wishbone. "We had chicken last night. You want to make a wish."

I grab an end. I wish that Mrs. Sherwood was dead, then I pull.

Bobby wins.

"What'd you wish for?"

"I wished my parents weren't going to Florida," he says, then turns to look out the window.

"I didn't mean it. I fell asleep."

"You shouldn't've played with my stuff."

"Can I come up now?"

"No. You can't ever come up again."

"I'll never do it again, I promise."

He strips off a piece of bark and throws it. I pick up the bark and throw it back.

"You better watch out."

"Says who?"

"Says me."

I watch him from the corner of my eye as I pick up a stick.

"You'd better not," he warns.

I look up, then throw the stick at him.

"All right, you're going to get it now." He starts down the tree.

I squeal and start running. I pump my legs, running as fast as I can. I come to the edge of the woods and know I'm safe.

As soon as I think that, something smashes into my back and knocks me to the ground. I roll into a ball.

"Don't hit me!" I shout.

"You started it."

"I'll tell," I threaten.

"Little baby's going to tell his mommy," John mimics.

I roll over to my back and look up at him. "C'mon, John, don't," I plead.

"Get up," he says, and starts back to his fort.

I wait until he's ten feet away before I pick up a stick and throw it at him. It hits him in the back.

"You've had it now!" he shouts.

"I didn't mean it," I scream, and take off.

He catches me on the edge of our back yard. He thumps me on the back. I fall to the ground. I can't breathe.

"You okay?" John kneels beside me.

I gasp, then draw in a huge mouthful of air and stagger to my feet. "I'm going to tell."

"Go ahead and tell. I don't care," John says. He kicks some dirt at me. I sniffle, then start toward the house.

John darts around me and charges inside. "He started it, he was throwing things at me!" he yells.

My mother is in front of the stove. When she turns, she's wearing her sunglasses.

"Mom?" John starts towards her.

"What did you do to your brother?"

John steps back in surprise.

"Isn't there enough hitting going on around here, without you two..." My mother suddenly stops. She shakes her head and turns away.

"Mom..." John moves to her. He touches her shoulder.

My mother whips around. For a moment I'm afraid she's going to hit him, but then she crouches and wraps her arms around him. She's crying. I can see the tears coming from beneath her sunglasses.

"You can't hit," she says softly, still holding John.

I move to her side. She hugs me with her other arm.

"You can not hurt each other," she says, then sobs.

"Mommy," I whisper, and start to cry.

There's ice along the edges of the lake. Nancy's wearing blue jeans, a green sweater, and a red jacket with a hood. She picks up a piece of ice and licks it.

"Bobby's parents are going to Florida."

"Tallahassee," she says quickly.

I grin, then stoop over to pick up a flat rock. I skip it across the water.

She picks up a rock and throws.

We skip rocks until there's no more flat ones left. We climb the fence and walk over to the summer houses. When we sit on the edge of the pier, Nancy wants to hold my hand.

"How come?"

"We're engaged."

"So what?"

"So that means we have to hold hands."

"Not all the time," I say quickly. "Not at school."

"No, just when no one's around."

I let her hold my hand. Her fingers are cold.

"I told my mother I was going to marry you."

"What'd she say?"

"She said that was nice."

I nod and peel off a splinter from the pier. I throw it in the water and watch it drift away.

"You want me to kiss you?"

"No," I say, making a face.

"Okay. You want to go over to your father's boat?"

I stand up and try to pull my hand away, but she won't let go.

"Let go, somebody's going to see us."

"Nobody's going to...."

I put my fingers to my lips. I pull her with me as I run behind one of the summer houses.

We peek around the corner of the house. Barry Miller and Joyce are walking along the lake. They're holding hands. Nancy grins at me.

Barry and Joyce walk out to the end of the pier.

Nancy giggles as Barry puts his arm around Joyce's shoulders. Joyce leans her head against his neck.

We crouch beside the building and peek around the edge.

Barry kisses Joyce right on the mouth.

"Wow!" Nancy whispers.

Barry's hand slides under Joyce's sweater and keeps moving.

"What's he doing now?"

"I don't know."

Joyce's legs close around Barry's, then he rolls on top of her.

"Are they wrestling?"

"I don't think so," Nancy answers. She's staring at Barry and Joyce. Her eyes are very big.

When I look back, Barry's pulling up Joyce's sweater.

"Look at that," I say, as Joyce's stomach pops out.

Barry reaches down and does something to the top of Joyce's pants.

"He's taking her pants off," I say in surprise.

Nancy glares at me.

Barry suddenly stops. He looks up at the summer house. "Who's up there?"

Nancy giggles. I start laughing, too.

Barry yells and starts up the hill.

We run out to the road and all the way to the field and hide by the apple tree.

"What do you think he was doing?"

Nancy shrugs.

"I don't think you're supposed to do that."

"Do what?"

"Take off Joyce's pants. I don't think you can do that."

"Why not?"

"It's cold. She could get sick."

"It is cold." Nancy wraps her arms around her knees.

I look at her from the corner of my eye, thinking about Joyce's stomach, remembering the dark patch of hair on my mother's stomach.

When I raise my glance, Nancy's looking at me.

I blush and look away.

Her hand creeps over to mine. Her hand is very hot.

We don't say anything. We walk through the field, then stop and turn off the path. We push our way into the weeds. I stomp down the weeds until I've made a small circle. We both sit down. It feels as if we're far away from everyone.

"You go first."

"I don't want to."

"You said you would."

"You started it."

Nancy looks at me for a moment, then takes off her coat.

"Are you cold?"

"It's warm in here." She grins then wraps her arms around her chest. She looks at me, then pulls her sweater over her head. She's wearing a white t-shirt.

"You take off yours now."

"Maybe we shouldn't do this," I say, thinking about Mr. Helke, thinking he might get mad at me and not let me help him change his oil anymore.

"I won't tell."

"I won't either."

I pull off my jacket, then take off my shirt.

Nancy leans over to examine me.

"You look just like me," she says. She pulls her t-shirt off. Her chest is just like mine. I don't feel so bad now. I reach for my shirt.

"What about the rest?"

"You mean our pants, too?"

"I will if you will."

"I don't want to do that." I pick up my shirt and pull it on. I'm doing the buttons, when Nancy says, "I dare you."

And I say, "I double dare you."

Nancy bites her lip, then reaches down and unzips her jeans. She leans back and rolls them down her legs.

I crouch over to look. Her underpants are different from mine. They're all smooth in front.

"Now you," she says.

I hesitate.

"I triple dare you," she whispers. Her voice is shaky.

I take a deep breath, then pull my pants down to my knees.

"Wow," Nancy says. "Yours are different."

She touches the front of my underwear. "How come it's like that?"

"So I can I go to the bathroom."

"Why don't you just pull them down."

"I don't have to."

"You don't!"

"No."

"I do," Nancy says.

"Why?" I say, and then Nancy shows me.

And then I show Nancy.

"John?"

"What?"

"How come Mrs. Helke never wears her sunglasses?"

"Because she isn't married to him."

I lie on my back and watch the shadows from John's flashlight.

"John?"

"What now?"

"How come you always call him, him?"

"Go to sleep."

"How come?"

John sighs, then rolls over on his side. His pajama tops are pushed up. I can see the bones sticking out of his back. There are four of them.

I fall asleep looking at my brother's bones, and dream about Nancy's stomach and how smooth it is between her legs.

25

I stagger into the clearing. Loony leaps to his feet.

"Where?" The word grates against my throat.

Loony gaze shifts nervously across my face. His 16 is raised and trained on the ground in front of me.

"Where is he!"

Loony steps back. "What are you doing, man?"

I swing the shotgun around until it's pointed at his chest.

"There. He's up there." He motions to the ledge above.

I turn, stagger, then right myself and start towards the path.

I whirl when I hear Loony start to follow.

"Wait here," I order.

"Just be cool, man," he says, backing away, holding his hands in front of him.

I start up the path.

I hear the girl singing and the soft murmur of Lester's voice.

I slide into the bramble and move silently towards the clearing, towards the circle of rocks.

"My daughter," Lester whispers.

I step into the clearing. For a moment all I see is Lester, standing over the little girl. His hand is on her shoulder. His other hand is hidden behind his back. She's smiling, looking up at him expectantly.

"I will never leave..." Lester stops abruptly as he catches sight of me.

"Where the fuck is he?" I demand, raising the shotgun.

He smiles. His hand gently closes around the girl's neck.

"He is safe now."

"Where is he?"

"All my sons are safe. No one will ever hurt them again," he says, then steps to the side. The little girl follows.

Hoang's body is on the ground. His throat is slashed. A pool of blood forms a dark halo around his head.

"What the fuck have you done?" I sob, dropping to my knees.

Lester moves to my side. He smiles tenderly, then reaches out.

I rear back from his touch.

"My child," Lester whispers. "I'll never leave you."

"No!" I scream and scramble to my feet.

The girl is singing. She skips forward, looks at Hoang's body, then turns to smile at me.

Lester reaches for her. His arm appears from behind his back.

I see a flash of light, Lester's gentle smile, and the girl's song is wrenched from her throat in a bright arc of blood.

"She is safe now," Lester murmurs.

The girls body dances on the ground.

I shake my head, trying to clear my eyes. "You can't do this. You...".

"My son." Lester holds out his arms and moves towards me.

"NO!" I scream, and swing the shotgun.

Lester pauses. He shakes his head sadly, and I pull the trigger.

I obliterate him. I fire, pump, fire again, until I wipe him from existence, until there's nothing left but the stink of cordite and my own screams.

Loony arms are clamped around my chest. He tries to pull me away. I throw back an elbow, feel it connect, hear him grunt.

I hunch forward, ripping at the earth.

The white bones slowly crawl from the graves until all the small delicate shards surround me, singing silently.

"Jesus fucking Christ!" Loony sobs.

I'm on my knees in the freshly turned earth. The six small skulls, carefully balanced on the edge of the hole, grin back at me vacantly.

"What the..." Loony shakes his head. He covers his face and turns away.

I listen to him cry as I turn and smile at the children's skulls.

I close my eyes.

I hear their song.

Coming into the valley, I realize I've lost my 16. I smile at Loony when he looks over his shoulder at me.

He grabs my arm and shoves me forward.

I stumble, then skip ahead. The bush parts to let me pass. I hear Loony cursing behind me.

We cower in the trees. Ahead of us are a group of men walking along the path.

I wave to them.

Loony jerks me to the ground. His hand closes around the back of my head and he pushes my face into the dirt.

I try to tell him I can't breath, but I start to smile, then I laugh.

I can't stop laughing.

I'm the only one who can hear it.

We cross the river. When we get to the other side, Loony reaches over and pulls down my pants. I watch curiously as he burns away fat black worms from my calves and thighs.

I stoop to look at them when he does the same for himself.

He grabs me by the arm and drags me away from the worms. I look back over my shoulder until I can no longer see the river.

I remember a lake.

I remember crayfish.

And I remember a girl.

I try to tell Loony about this. But he won't listen.

There are two men standing in the path. Loony and I are crouched to the side, watching them. The men are dressed in black pajamas. Loony says we have to be quiet. We're almost home.

"Where's home?" I whisper.

Loony glares at me.

"Are they our friends?" I ask, and stand up. "Hey, we're over here," I call.   The men turn. One of them has a gun.

Loony explodes behind me.

When I turn to look at him, he's on the ground. His chest is opened.

"Are you okay, Loony?" I kneel beside him, but he doesn't answer.

One of the men in pajamas walks over to me.

"Hi," I say. "Loony's hurt."

The man nudges Loony with his foot, then puts his gun against my forehead. I grin back at him and reach up to hold the barrel of the gun. It feels cold.

The other man starts to sing, then they are both singing to each other.

"Loony's hurt," I tell them again, but they turn and walk away without answering.

I sit with Loony until he stops moving.

When it gets dark, I start to walk.

I walk all night.

When it starts to get light, some men find me.

One of them holds my hand and says he'll take me home.

I'm in a white room in a white bed. People come to look at me. They stand around and watch me. Their eyes try to peel away my flesh to discover my secrets.

I want to tell them I don't have any secrets anymore, but I'm afraid.

They keep standing there, staring at me with their bullet eyes, daring me to say something.

26

"What's this?"

"My book report," I mumble.

"And what book did you say you read?"

"Pirate's Promise."

Mrs. Sherwood glares at me. I don't know what she wants me to say.

"And how many pages is Pirate's Promise?"

"I don't know." I look at the floor.

She makes a noise in her throat and picks up a book. It's Pirate's Promise. She opens it to the last page.

"It's sixty three pages long. And you're trying to tell me, you read all of those pages since Friday?"

"Yes."

"Why are you lying to me?"

"I'm not lying."

"You did not read this book, and I will not have you lie to me."

"But I did read it. I liked it," I say. "It's my favorite book."

She glares and starts tapping her finger on her desk. She has long fingernails, even longer than my mother's.

"I want you stand up here until you can admit to me, and the class, that you did not read this book."

"I read it, Mrs. Sherwood, honest I did."

"Don't you dare start crying."

Some of the kids snicker.

"Now you just stand there until you're man enough to admit that you lied."

Everyone is watching me. Mrs. Sherwood is talking about England. She stops to look over her shoulder. I shuffle my feet and look away.

"Are you ready to tell me the truth?"

"I told the truth. I read Pirate's Promise."

Mrs. Sherwood snorts and goes back to talking about England.

I look out the window and try to hate her harder. It makes my head hurt.

When the bell rings, Mrs. Sherwood makes me stay until everyone else is gone. I'm afraid I'll miss the bus.

"Are you ready now to tell me the truth?"

"I told the truth. Honest I did."

She shakes her head. "No, you didn't. You're lying to me, and I will not tolerate that."

"But..."

"And don't think for a minute that you're going to get away with it." She takes a deep breath. "Tomorrow you will stand in front of the class again, until you admit you lied."

"But I read it." I start to cry.

Mrs. Sherwood leans over her desk and says, "Wouldn't it be so much easier, if you just admitted that you never read the book."

"But I read it," I try to tell her, but I'm crying too hard.

Mrs. Sherwood looks at me and waits.

I take a deep breath, sniffle, then whisper, "I lied." and start crying again.

Mrs. Sherwood smiles, and tells me I can go home now.

As I walk out the door, I say, "I read Pirate's Promise, I did." but I say it very quietly so she can't hear me.

"...and she wouldn't let me sit down all day."

"It's okay," John says. "Don't cry." He punches me lightly on the shoulder.

"But she said I was a liar."

"She's crazy," John says.

"She is," I agree.

"It's Monday." John grins.

"Daddy's bowling!" I smile and wipe my eyes as we turn the block to our house.

John starts to tell me about the frogs in Mr. Thorpe's classroom, when he suddenly stops.

"What's wrong?"

He points to the house.

My father's car in the driveway.

"What's daddy doing home? He's supposed to be bowling."

John shakes his head and kicks a rock.

"Your father doesn't feel well," my mother says. She's wearing her sunglasses and she has on a big red sweater. The sleeves come all the way down to her hands.

"So I want both of you to be on your best behavior tonight. Okay?" She smiles brightly.

John doesn't say anything. My mother looks at him for a moment, then touches the side of his cheek.

"It's going to be all right," she says softly.

I look at both of them, trying to figure out what she's talking about.

When I go up to change, my father is in his chair. He has his newspaper in front of him. On the table beside him is his drink.

I change into jeans and a grey sweatshirt. When I come back down the stairs, my father lowers his newspaper and glares.

I slow down and move very quietly into the kitchen. I can feel his eyes on my back.

"What's wrong with Daddy?"

"He has a bug," my mother answers, without turning.

"What's for dinner?"

"Spaghetti."

"Where'd John go?"

"He went to get the mail." My mother puts the top back on the pot. She opens a cupboard.

"How was school?"

I feel my face get hot. "It was okay.,"

My mother nods and goes back to the stove.

"What's for dessert?"

"Brownies."

"Bobby was sick today."

"What was wrong with him?"

"He's got a bug," I say, then add, "Maybe it's daddy's bug."

John comes in with the mail.

"Did I get anything?"

"Why would you get anything," John sneers, and looks at my mother.

"Just put it on the counter," she says, without turning.

"We're having spaghetti," I tell him.

He shrugs and sits at the kitchen table.

"Daddy's got a bug," I say, and sit across from him.

"Edna?" my father yells.

My mother doesn't move. She stands so still it makes me laugh.

John glares at me.

"Edna?" my father calls again, more loudly.

My mother rushes into the other room.

When she returns, she's carrying my father's glass. We watch her refill it, then carry it out to my father.

"He must be very sick not to go bowling."

John doesn't say anything. He gets up and leaves the room. I hear his footsteps on the stairs.

"Here," Nancy says, and holds out her hand. She's wearing her red jacket and jeans.

"What is it?"

"It's a surprise. Hold out your hand and close your eyes."

I feel something drop in my palm. When I open my eyes, there's a gold ring in the center of my hand.

"Wow!" I slide the ring onto my finger.

"It's my favorite ring. My father gave it to me for my birthday last year."

"It's nice."

"That means we're going to get married," Nancy tells me.

"Not for a while."

"No," Nancy agrees. "Not until we get older."

I nod, looking at my new ring. It looks good on my finger.

Nancy leans over. She has her eyes closed and her lips are all puckered up.

I kiss her quickly and go back to looking at my ring.

"Look at this," I shout, as I spot John coming into the clearing. "Nancy gave it to me."

John looks at the ring, then at Nancy.

"It means we're going to get married," Nancy tells him, and blushes.

"Good luck," he mutters, and kicks the trunk of the tree.

"You want to come up?"

John shrugs, then shinnies up to our branch. He sits with his back against the trunk.

"Where's Terry and Randy?"

"I don't know." John peels a stick from the branch and breaks it into little pieces. He throws it to the ground. We all watch it fall.

"We're having spaghetti for dinner," I tell Nancy.

"Spaghetti's my favorite," she says. "Maybe I can eat at your house."

"No!" John says, before I can answer.

"Why not?" I ask.

"Just no," John says again. He swings to the ground and walks up the path toward the house.

"How come he said that?" Nancy asks. "Doesn't he like me?"

"He likes you a lot."

"Honest?"

"Honest," I say, then hang upside down by my legs. "Bet you can't do this?"

Nancy swings down until she's hanging beside me. I start to tickle her until she makes me stop.

"What are you doing?"

John's standing in front of the sink, staring at the wall.

He doesn't answer. I touch his shoulder. He's starting to scare me.

He whirls and slaps my hand away.

"I didn't do anything."

His face is very red. It almost looks like he's going to cry.

"How come you told Nancy she couldn't..." I stop when I hear her voice. It's coming from their bedroom.

She's screaming.

"What's he doing to her?"

John leans over the sink. His hands curl into fists.

I hear my father shouting.

Their voices are very loud. My mother is crying.

"He's hurting her again," I moan, and look at John.

John sobs, then whips around and races by me. He runs down the hall, and without stopping slams into my parent's door.

"Leave her alone!" John yells.

I run down to the bedroom and peek around the corner.

My mother is lying on the bed. Her sunglasses are hanging from one of her ears and she's bleeding.

My father is at the edge of the bed. He has his hands on his hips, and he's staring at John.

"What did you say to me?"

"Leave her alone," John says so softly I can barely hear him.

"Go back in the kitchen," my mother cries. She's biting her lip. There's blood on her nose and chin.

My father's eyes are bullets. He takes a step towards John.

John doesn't move.

"Or what?" my father taunts.

"Just leave her alone," John says, and moves to my mother's side.

My father laughs, then suddenly lashes out and slaps John across the face.

John staggers against the bed.

My mother tries to grab him, but he ducks away and glares at my father.

My father laughs.

"John," I whisper.

"John!" my mother shrieks.

John throws himself at my father. He punches him in the stomach.

My father sneers, then picks him up by the back of his shirt and throws him against the wall.

I take a step into the room. No one notices me.

My father moves towards John.

John stumbles to his feet. He charges my father.

My mother screams. My father laughs as he punches John in the chest.

John falls on the floor and doesn't move.

I run over to his side. I can't stop crying. My parents are screaming at each other. I keep touching John's shoulder. I think he's dead.

My mother sobs. I hear my father slapping her.

"John, don't die," I whisper. "Please, don't die."

"Don't you ever do that again," my father yells, and I hear him hit her again.

John groans and turns on his side.

"Where is he?" he grunts.

"Are you okay?" I'm still crying.

John stumbles to his feet and runs out of the room.

"You again," I hear my father snort, then hear the sound of someone falling.

By the time I get to the living room, my father is standing over John.

John is on the floor. My mother is on the couch with her face in her hands. Her hands are all bloody.

"All of you make me fucking sick!" my father screams, then goes into the kitchen. I hear the clicking sound of his bottles.

Everyone's crying. My father is sitting in his chair drinking.

"Hold him," John tells me. His eye is black and blue and his lip is swollen.

I grab Prince and John slips the rope around his neck.

"I hate all of you!" John screams.

"You make me sick!" I yell, then we push Prince out of the fort.

He whimpers for a long time, and then he stops.

Mrs. Sherwood leaves me alone. She doesn't say anything to me all day.

Right before the bell rings, I walk up to her desk. I don't say anything.

"What do you want?"

I look at the clock. In six seconds the bell will ring.

I say, "I read Pirate's Promise, and it's my favorite book."

Before she can say anything, the bell rings.

I run out of the classroom and out to the bus.

My father is very nice to us. He makes a joke and my mother laughs.

My father looks at John and waits for him to laugh.

John says he has to do his homework and goes upstairs.

My father shakes his head and looks at me.

I look back and wait for him to tell me a joke.

He picks up his drink and turns to my mother.

She smiles and says, "It'll be all right. He just needs some time."

My father doesn't say anything, he just touches her leg.

My mother smiles and holds his hand.

"You have to be very quiet."

"Where are we going?"

"I want to show you something?"

"What?"

"You'll see." I take him through the field out to the road. It's starting to get dark. I hope we're not too late.

We come to the edge of the property. I crouch then run to the side of the house. I look back at the road and wave to John.

He runs over and crouches beside me.

"What are we doing?" he whispers.

I grin, then take his hand and lead him around to the other side of the house. We duck below the windows until we come to the one I want.

"Look," I say, and stand on my toes. Mr. Helke, Mrs. Helke, and Nancy are sitting around their dining room table.

Nancy's laughing and telling a story.

Mrs. Helke grins. Mr. Helke rolls his eyes and makes everyone laugh.

Nancy reaches for a potato and drops her fork on the floor.

Mr. Helke bends over to pick it up for her. When he hands it to her, he grins and touches her arm.

"Did you see that," I whisper in disbelief.

I hear Nancy's laughter all the way through the window.

John groans.

I start to turn.

He shoves me away and runs across the yard.

"What's wrong?" I call, but he keeps running.

I run after him through the darkness, following the sound of his cries.

I come to a halt at the edge of the clearing beneath my brother's fort. John is kneeling in the center of it.

He's crying.

I start crying too.

Prince is still hanging from the tree.

John is kneeling below him. He keeps saying, I'm sorry over and over again.

He's crying, and I don't know what to do.

27

I write:

I'm coming home. They say I don't belong here. I don't think anybody does.

Then I sign my name.

After a while, I add a postscript.

I write:

Do you remember Prince?

Do you remember what we did?